What Readers Are Saying About *Da Vinci's Way*

"While girls are currently underrepresented in STEM, Charley brings in a new perspective with *Da Vinci's Way*. She is quirky, relatable, and passionate about exploring and learning. Her journey is compelling. Cannot wait for the next adventure!"

—Kirthi Kumar, 16, founder, SheSoft Foundation

"Contributing to the interactive web platform for the Edge of Yesterday book series these past two years has helped me see how STEM and the humanities are interconnected in our world."

—Lindsay Bernhards, intern, Edge of Yesterday

"I remember reading one of the drafts of Charley's next adventure and not being able to look away from the page. I am in awe that I lent a hand in the creation of her next time-travel adventure, and I can't wait for readers to be transported, just like Charley, into Leonardo's Italy."

—Claire van Stolk, 18, intern, Edge of Yesterday

"*Da Vinci's Way* has given me so many new opportunities to write about and explore things I love and am interested in, like history, art, Italian culture, and even fashion. By writing articles for the Edge of Yesterday website that connect to the books, I learn much more than I would in a classroom."

—Hannah D   lge of Yesterday

"I enjoyed reading more abo   Renaissance man himself, Leonardo da Vi   :l like you are journeying back to the late 14uus in a story packed with adventure, and keeps you intrigued to know what Charley is going to do next!"

—Ava Brandstatter, 12

Also by Robin Stevens Payes

Edge of Yesterday, Book I

Da Vinci's Way

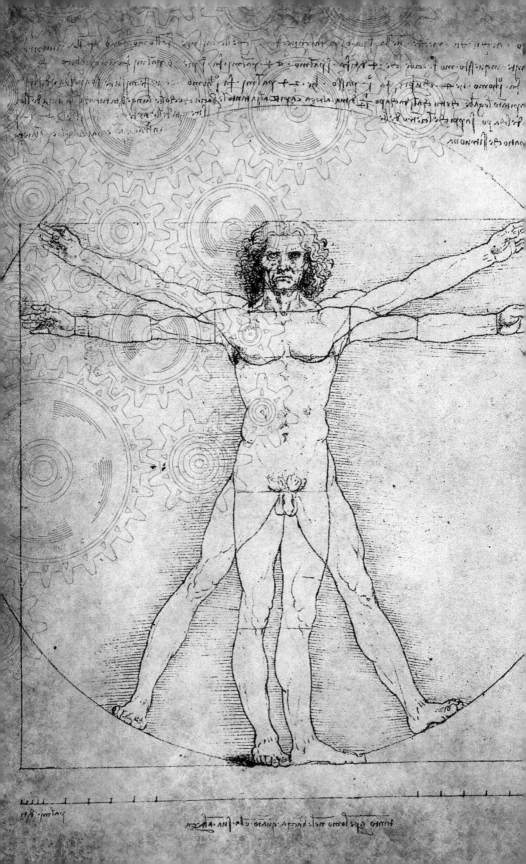

Da Vinci's Way

Edge of Yesterday
Book II

Printed in the United States of America.

Cover design by Melissa Brandstatter
Interior design by Lisa Vega
Layout composition by Megan Katsanevakis

Author bio photo by Judy Gee

Map image, page 70, courtesy of MyReadingMapped/Google
Globe image, page 71 © Washington Map Society
Other images courtesy of Creative Commons/Wikimedia
and Robin Stevens Payes

Library of Congress Control Number: 2018946463
ISBN: 978-1-937650-93-3

SMALL
BATCH
BOOKS

493 SOUTH PLEASANT STREET
AMHERST, MASSACHUSETTS 01002
413.230.3943

SMALLBATCHBOOKS.COM

To my parents, for the questions: What is art? What lies beyond the stars?
To Joel, for questing after social justice and also for accepting what is.
For these foundations at the edge of yesterday, I am deeply grateful.

"Learn how to see. Realize that everything is connected to everything else."

—Leonardo da Vinci

Contents

CHARLEY'S SPARKNOTES ON *EDGE OF YESTERDAY*: THE PAST IS PRESENT

HERE'S WHERE THINGS GET REALLY CRAZY

Dear reader, my adventure has begun with a bang. An unexpected trip to the deep past, thanks to a time machine that Leonardo da Vinci himself designed. The genius da Vinci could imagine it, but it took a middle school science fair assignment—and me and Billy, my science fair partner and Da Vinci Middle School's geekiest eighth grade brain—to build it!

But then Lex had to mess up our plans. He's our school's star athlete and *il gorgioso*. Worse, he knows it.

So, it is not without some embarrassment that I confess that I, too, may have been seduced by his charm. An accidental kiss, a slip, and a flip of the switch turned on our temporal accelerator and accidentally sent me spiraling (literally—it was like riding a roller coaster while being tossed in a clothes dryer!) to a deep past five hundred years before I was born—with no way to get home.

Then, out of the blue, I find myself face-to-face with my Florentine idol, Leonardo da Vinci. True story!

I, Charley Morton, girl scientist-musician-soccer player and all-round polymath (a great spelling bee practice word for, like, a Renaissance genius, although I'm also just a normal teen with big dreams), have built a time machine spurred on by a drawing, a dream, and a school project. Even I couldn't imagine it actually working. Now I'm stuck in some faraway land. It's like a bad fairytale. I have no idea what the future holds for me here or, in fact, what future I can even look forward to.

When, out of the blue, I find myself face-to-face with my Florentine idol, Leonardo da Vinci.

I know I have accomplished something BIG. How big? Only time will tell.

It is only now, when Leonardo has disappeared into the inky night to retrieve his inventions—weapons for Lorenzo de' Medici's defense of Florence . . . missiles that I have seen da Vinci's designs for in my own time—that I have a moment to catch my breath. Luckily, the torch the Maestro staked on the ground before me to illumine this very spot a few moments ago still burns bright enough that I can scribble my thoughts here in my spiral for a private blog to Billy—because there is no one else who would believe what has happened. Not even my parents. ESPECIALLY not my parents! If Billy gets it and decides to leak it—for my safety and your amazement—well, I cannot be held accountable for actions in a future I may have all but disappeared from!

Or maybe I won't even exist. . . .

Notes of a once and (hopefully) future American teen to a current and always-present American teen (a.k.a. Billy Vincenzo, trusted science fair partner and brainiac):
1. I am alive and breathing ancient air. Clean—or not?

2. Time machine worked!

3. May have hacked space-time continuum. What are the chances of that?

4. Really rough ride. Think: tornado combined with earthquake combined with volcanic eruption. Then being popped like popcorn. And that's just the half of it.

5. Lex is a real jerk. NEVER trust the studliest guy in school to have more than his own interests at heart.

6. I met LEONARDO da friggin' VINCI for reals!

7. I can't wait to ask him all my questions about how he could do everything, learn everything, and get to BE the Ultimate Renaissance Man.

8. Praying that some echo of this can bounce to the present—er, future—to alert you to our amazing, unbelievable, awe-inspiring accomplishment: time travel!

If I can, I will type this up later as a blog and try to send it to Billy—that's a BIG IF. It seems a bit like putting a random message in a bottle in the middle of the ocean. Or random digits in the middle of space-time! What was I thinking about when I came up with this idea—that I'd just bounce my signals up to a GPS satellite? I mean, Charley, dummy, there are no satellites in the fifteenth century. For all I know, Columbus still sails the ocean blue . . . at the distant edge of the known world. A lot like me!

So, if this post reaches Billy once I try to send it later today—I mean in *my* today, that is, my once and (hopefully) future space-time dimension—what will he even make of it?

To tell the truth, I'm pretty scared. I mean, this whole thing is so much bigger than me. And my whole body's beginning to ache. I wonder if I might have some Advil floating in the bottom of my backpack, but I'm too tired to even look.

I begin to shake. The strange landscape suddenly blurs as my eyes well up, but I screw up my courage and set my mind—now that I'm here, I've got to complete my mission!

But I feel so alone. Who ever could imagine our invention would actually work!

What am I supposed to do now?! I survived a major time shift, but will I survive this wild place and be able to learn from Leonardo—and even scarier, will I ever get home again?

Stay tuned, dear reader, 'cause the pit in my gut says the real test is just beginning.

I.

DISCOVERING THE OLD WORLD

The cannonball, the fall, l'Uomo Universale—it's like I've been in this situation before, but how can that be? There is nothing even remotely familiar in these surroundings.

I smell something like gunpowder, even though I've never really smelled gunpowder. What else could it be, this acrid stench? And after the cannonball rolled by my foot—and then I tried to move and felt my ankle start to throb. . . .

This cannot be real, Charley.

I wipe the drip from my eyes. No tears! I look at my hands—grimy with soot and dirt. In my backpack, I find a crumpled tissue and use that to wipe off some of the schmutz. (This is a Yiddish word that means dirt or grime. It somehow sounds more descriptive when you say it out loud, *sch-mutz.* Try it!) Then I notice my tablet. You know how, on airplanes, they say that things may have shifted during landing? Well . . . same. I'm just hoping that doesn't refer to cracked screens on my devices.

I cautiously lift the cover. There's dust all over the screen, but it's intact! I take a swipe at it with the now-dirty Kleenex and insert the tablet gently into my backpack. "Keep working . . . keep working . . . keep on working!" I beg the device. It suddenly feels like a lifeline to reality—whatever that is.

I take one last peek under the cover—the lock screen lights up reassuringly. Settled, I breathe a bit easier.

"*Al diavolo!*" bellows a loud, deep voice. I jump up as I hear heavy rumbling coming up from behind; my gimp foot strikes the ground, sending up shooting waves of pain. I suddenly see stars, and my whole body tenses—I can't take any more surprises.

"*Ecco*, Carlotta!"

"Huh?" So I wasn't dreaming. Here is Leonardo da Vinci himself, cursing and calling out to me.

I squint and wink first one eye, then the other. One eye is still blurry, but at least I can open it a bit wider now.

Ser Leonardo (as I expect the one-and-only Leonardo da Vinci would be called) is approaching in my direction, tugging at a heavy rope, straining from the weight of a weird-looking, iron cannon-like thingy mounted on a cart. I recognize it from a drawing in one of the da Vinci codices (plural for *codex*—meaning notebook), as one of his inventions: a triple-barreled cannon.

Weird. Who would believe that his designs for wildly future inventions might ever be constructed in Leonardo's day and age, much less actually work many centuries before their time?

But I am apparently proof that, whatever Ser Leonardo imagined, he could build—for now I have become history's first verifiable time traveler. His design for a time machine has brought me from the twenty-first century five hundred years back in time.

No mean feat for a fifteenth-century artist, dreamer, and inventor.

Da Vinci, that is.

Now that I have achieved my own unlikely goal of meeting the world's original Renaissance genius, I have to figure out where I am, how I actually got here, and what to do while I'm here. And how to get back/wake up/get out of this reality show in time for the science fair. (Oh, did I mention: This all started out as part of a crazy, cockamamy scheme for the middle school science fair?)

Surveying the situation, I have to accomplish this feat with a maybe-broken ankle, a black eye, some random modern (for my time) high-tech gear that may or may not work here—wherever *here* actually turns out to be—and a handful of red, yellow, and green gummy worms to keep my tummy from rumbling.

Normally, I would use my senses—and my sense of reason—to figure out where I am and what the situation calls for. Unfortunately, panic, pain, hunger, and extreme disorientation have stripped me of my powers of reason. In biology, we learned that this triggers the primal "fight, freeze, or flight" response, like our ancient ancestors felt when a saber-toothed tiger was charging them.

Nonsense, Charley—you are not in danger of being mauled by wolves. (*But here is danger!* the voice inside my head shouts.) Just take some deep breaths. . . .

"We must get your ankle wrapped up, *cara*."

Leonardo da Vinci's words first come to my ears as so much "blah, blah, blah," but luckily, I have Translator—an invention that provides immediate translation from Italian to English, and vice versa—which lets me communicate here (unlike in Bruegel's painting of the Tower of Babel, where no one understood each other).

"*Cara*," he said. I look around wondering who the Maestro would call "dear," until I realize he's talking to me! He carries a length of linen smudged with paint and smelling of pine trees. I wrinkle my nose to remember this scent—turpentine—and it comes to me: This must be an artist's rag he uses for painting. He motions to me to sit. "You will need both legs to walk into Firenze."

"Firenze, *si*!" I say, peering through the darkness to register that this is, indeed, my current location. Something niggles at me about the idea of Florence—a feeling there is something else about this place. But my head hurts too much to call that to mind.

I try to concentrate on the here and now.

As he artfully wraps my foot in the smelly cloth, Ser Leonardo begins rapid-fire instructions telling me how to get to his atelier. (Translator helpfully indicates this is a French word meaning artist's studio or workshop.) "You must walk through this field, ascend the ramp, and you'll find my studio at the top, over the tavern, *va bene!*"—all in Italian-accented Latin, or maybe Latinized Italian. Even with Translator and the rudiments (definition: basics) of a first-year Italian vocabulary, I am lost trying to follow directions. We all know, at best, I am "directionally challenged." And here, now, I am far from being at my best.

"*Adagio, molto adagio!*" I tell him over and over, then wonder if this is only a post-Renaissance musical notation for "slow down." I can't keep up when someone's talking really fast—like, apparently, Leonardo when he's excited. Like now.

Unexpectedly, I hear a horse's hooves pounding from a distance and someone shouting, "Signorina!" I turn around to a familiar face. Live and in person.

"Kairos!"

His horse circles around me once, twice, before he pulls in the reins to halt his steed.

"At your service, *bella* Carlotta!"

I want to hug him—I'm so relieved to see a familiar face—but the horse and Leonardo stand in my way. I hop up on my good foot with what I'm sure is the silliest grin. "Kairos, I'm here! Me and the great da Vinci! And you!"

Leonardo looks from me to Kairos and back. "She is . . . ?" he begins, Kairos nodding in assent. "You have . . . ? *Puella ex machina est!*"

The girl from the machine.

"*Si,* Maestro! You did not miscalculate. The technology of the future is a marvel!" Kairos beams at me.

This adds to my confusion. "You're . . . ? So you meant me to . . . I mean you chose *me* to come here? How come?"

"Perchè no?" Leonardo exclaims. "You are curious. And smart. We also! Kindred spirits *ex tempora.* Out of time."

I think back to my first meeting with Kairos—during Take Your Child to Work Day at Dad's office last week (or five-hundred-plus years from now, I remind myself). At first I thought he was someone's kid, there for the experience—he looked not that much older than me, although there are those who tell me I'm thirteen going on thirty. Then it seemed like he was some super-smart IT dude. And he admitted to being from another place. But this place?

"Show him, Carlotta! The magic slate you carry in your sack!" Kairos urges me. "Maestro, your wish is Carlotta's command. The world in a sack." Leonardo crowds closer, and I wonder whether I am not here to teach the master.

I unzip my backpack and start to sort through the junk inside: Solar battery, check. Lego bot servomotors, check. Gummy worms, check. Thank goodness I grabbed the backpack before Lex accosted me. (Guys and the games they play. Don't get me started!)

And therein, a bit of modern sustenance! I pull out the pack, extracting a single candy worm and suck in the familiar sugary sweetness.

A measure of calm returns, allowing me to think. What else is in here? I've forgotten. Cell phone, check. How the phone got in here, I can't remember for the life of me. I gently pull out my tablet, checking once again to make sure it's still working, and it lights up. But this is weird: The time it shows no longer ticks by in exquisitely precise and uniform digits; an hourglass has replaced it.

When he notices the screen light up, Leonardo reaches out and touches the tablet reverently. *"Un dispositivo di conteggio?"*

"Um, well it can be used for counting. Among other things," I reply, thinking that to explain to the original Renaissance genius what a modern-day polymath like Steve Jobs did in creating this device could take the next five hundred years.

"Hard landing?" Kairos asks, examining my bruises.

Before I can tell the story of my dramatic entry, Leonardo breaks in. "How would she even know to find me here?" Leonardo asks. "Except for *il Magnifico*, all of Italy believes I am in Milano. After all, this is *Anno Domini millequattrocento novantadue.*"

I don't get much of this besides the nickname for Lorenzo de' Medici—the ruler of Florence—and the city of Milan, and I'm guessing it's the year—hard to decipher, but I register it as 1492. I look around, squinting through the darkness to find a familiar landmark, but we appear to be in a countryside marked only by rolling hills, fields, and trees.

But the year . . . if it's 1492, what would be happening? Columbus— New World landing: check. Renaissance in full swing: check. Inquisition begins—oh no!

And Leonardo da Vinci—according to my own research, he should not be in Florence. His old patron Lorenzo de' Medici sent him off to work for the duke of Milan, Ludovico Sforza, a decade earlier. He should be building that gigantic horse sculpture . . . unless the Milanese are back at war and need the bronze for cannons.

Coincidence? Or could that be why Leo's here testing his inventions of war?

Kairos claps me a little too energetically on the shoulder; the push almost topples me over. I feel the sting of my foot as I try to regain my balance.

"A happy coincidence, Maestro," Kairos grins.

"That it is coincidence, I am not certain," Leonardo replies. "But of this, I am sure: Carlotta cannot remain here. What if she were to be seen like this, Kairos?! *Il Magnifico* is already unhappy that I have missed his deadline for this confounded experiment in nocturnal warfare. I have barely been able to shoot my tri-barreled cannon to prove its superior firepower, much less improve its trajectory. I cannot disappoint further—not if I expect another commission from my patron."

I feel something nudging me next to my ear and find that Kairos's horse has detected the gummy worm source and is attempting to lick those remaining out of their cellophane bag.

As I attempt to pull the sugary treat out of his way, my gimp foot again hits the ground, sending a shooting pain up my leg. "Yowzers!"

"Shh!" Leonardo pulls my arm around his shoulder to steady me. "They may hear you! Kairos, you must find the apothecary at once; tell the man he's to meet Carlotta at my atelier. I have instructed her where to go."

As he sees my confusion, Kairos pipes in with a mindware explanation—a pause after each hurried pronouncement by the Master.

"He's trying to reassure you. He means to say, 'Do not fear, Carlotta. You are here to learn, are you not? And learn you shall, even as you may teach us much! But the way is not without danger. There are those who will condemn you for knowing too much.'"

This does not seem to be an accurate translation. Leonardo is looking me up and down, looking for all the world like a disapproving father. He shakes his head. "Your dress is entirely unsuitable."

It's then I realize I'm still wearing the secondhand dress I thought would turn heads at the library—that ended up turning Lex's head quite a bit more than I imagined! I recognize my attempts at being fashion-forward seem a bit out of place now—even if I weren't mud-spattered. I can hear Beauty Queen Beth lecturing me on how tacky I look in this dress—in front of the painter of the *Mona Lisa*, no less. Oh, have I mentioned? Beth's my bestie—or was. We used to share everything. But ever since she's turned her substantial brain power to those typical teen girl obsessions—boys and clothes—we have nothing to say to each other. Sad.

So that begs the question of what *would* be appropriate. The only frame of reference I have is from the art of the Renaissance masters featuring curvy, voluptuous nudes or sexy shepherdesses, or demurely draped Madonnas (as in Mary, Jesus's mother, not the rock star), or noblewomen in embroidered, close-fitting caps and pleated neo-Greek gowns.

But what, for a normal girl like me?

I am seized again with panic. What am I doing here, anyway? Kairos must see my legs shaking as his horse clip-clops closer and begins to nuzzle me again, tickling my neck. He sticks his long, rough tongue out and manages this time to lick the gummy worm in my hand. I giggle despite myself and pull his nuzzle toward me, stroking it. It is comforting to know a horse is a horse, no matter what the century.

"You recognize my animal?" Kairos asks, using a warmer voice than I have yet heard from him.

I shake my head. I've only ever seen any of this as a computer hologram that I never quite thought of as real . . . except, I guess, for Kairos. Da Vinci was a guy from history. Though here I must add that Leonardo's supposed self-portraits do turn out to be quite a good likeness. But of course they would.

Kairos looks disappointed. "You don't recognize this snout"—here he pulls up his horse's nose—"and this?" He points to his own face and I mentally flash on the *modello*.

"It's . . . you're . . . he's . . . ?"

I root through my backpack once more and my hands close in on a newspaper-wrapped miniature sculpture. Yes, it's in here! I carefully draw out what then seemed a novelty, given to me in another time by one self-proclaimed alien, a.k.a. Kairos. Unwrapping the newspaper slowly, I note thankfully that the sculpture has survived this wild ride intact.

Kairos nods. "Carlotta, fear not. You will be safe as long as you follow the Maestro's commands."

I feel like a weight's been lifted off me. Kairos, the formula, the golden compass, the maquette. I would think it was destiny—*il destino*—if I believed in the irrational, illogical evolution of a universe in which time may flow in any direction. Which I don't, of course. At least, I think I don't.

But Leonardo, on seeing his mini opus, grows even more impatient. "Show no one these treasures of yours, Carlotta. You will be in grave danger! If they were to find you here . . . it will be light before long, and we must keep your secrets safe.

"So go—now, *sbrigati*! You will find the wife of the tavern keeper below my studio. Signora Vincenzo, by name. She has four daughters and servant girls of various sizes and shapes. She will be able to find you suitable clothing. And you have not eaten?"

I'm embarrassed to think he must hear my tummy growling. After all, I have not traveled five hundred years across six time zones without feeling a pit in my stomach. Gummy worms are not gonna cut it. "Ah, *si*, Ser Leonardo! *Buon appetito!*"

"*Va bene*, Kairos!" Leonardo commands. "Fetch the apothecary at once. Do not share with our good doctor any of the true details of your mission, lest he suspect strange occurrences. Know—he will not be happy to be wakened from his slumbers, but you must get her salves and dressings so there will be no swelling to the brain."

The brain! I touch my head gently, feeling the start of a good bump on the forehead. Yowee!

I start to say, "Let's pick up a hot-and-cold pack and ibuprofen at the

CVS"—but then I remember where I am.

Kairos circles his trusty steed close again and taps me on the head, reminding me of Translator. "Remember to listen carefully to all voices around you. You will be able to tune in to all you need to hear," he whispers.

Before I can respond, Leo slaps Kairos's horse on the rump to send my friend out of time and into the night.

"And you!" I quickly come to my senses as Leonardo turns back to me, waves those artist's hands with those long, amazing fingers, and warns, "*La vedova* Vincenzo will be tending the fires soon: You must hasten there before dawn to avoid suspicion."

"But what do I say if she asks where I've come from?"

"Tell her you are Kairos's English cousin. You speak only the language of the British Isles. And do not share any of your strange intelligence with others. If they learn of your powers, those religious men of great power will stop at nothing to destroy you—and your knowledge."

"The powers that be would destroy . . . me? But what threat am I to them?"

"You see the future. And it is unlikely to please those who want to control our knowledge of how things really work! So be stealthy with your strange tablet," Leonardo warns, as he removes his cape to wrap it around my shoulders.

Smoothing my hair from my face with fingers that seem to know every bone and hollow, he throws the hood over my head. It's way too big; I feel like the disappearing girl, lost in its folds.

Blinded momentarily, I push back the hood as my fingers feel for a tie or buckle to fasten it more securely. Just then, I feel a tap on my behind. I turn to see Leo pointing, and I hobble off in the darkness on a path that will lead I know not where.

II.
Do You Take American Express?

The distance is longer than I imagined, especially with my bum foot, no moonlight, and certainly no electric lights. There are no people here. I pull Translator down around my neck—the better to hear.

Although my eyes have adjusted somewhat to the night, the swelling around my eye makes it harder to see where I'm going. I stumble over every rock and tree root, landing on my bottom more than once. It's discouraging. It takes a moment to regain enough energy to move on. I can't help but look up at the vastness of the sky and wonder how I got here. Though I know I must hurry, in a way, I'm glad: Who ever saw so many stars!

I cannot stop to stargaze now; I'm in danger—or so Leonardo informs me. For a girl used to suburban whirs like air conditioners and cars, these strange night sounds—a hooting owl, the moo of a cow, a wolf howling in the distance—conspire to keep me moving.

I fit Translator safely back over my ears to muffle these inhuman sounds. Besides, its muffs are warm and there's a chill breeze blowing into the folds of the cape.

I spy the stars glittering off the Arno River, which I see is not more than ten yards from me, and lick my parched lips. I wish I'd thought to bring a filtered water bottle. Who knows whether it's safe to drink from the river!

As I approach the bridge, I spy two men idling by the road, one holding the lead of a mule. My brain registers the order, *Hide!* But I'm too tired, and besides, I am lost. Maybe they can confirm I'm going in the right direction. Or at least they might have a canteen of fresh water I can sip.

"Scusi?" I say tentatively.

The strangers apparently are waiting for such a moment. The first guy limps over with a smile.

"Eh, signorina. What is one *si bella* doing out at this tender hour?"

I curtsy, as I did with Leonardo. *"Scusi, Signor. Dov'è la casa di Vincenzo, vi prego?"*

I am not too tired to notice the look he exchanges with his compadre. "Aha! Antonio, it is Vincenzo she is looking for! Shall we lead her there?"

Antonio comes closer, leading his mule. I wish I could throw myself on that animal and ride. My feet are hurting! I knew I should've worn my Nikes instead of these stupid ballet flats. *"Oh no! Sneakers with that outfit?"* I can imagine Bethy lecturing me. I feel a pang. Where's Bethy now?

"Eh, perché no? Vincenzo is on our way, no?" He grabs me by the arm with a leering grin.

Fatigue or no, I swat at his face, screaming as loud as I can: "Let go of me! *STULTUS ASINUS! Stupido!"*

"This one is lively," Antonio grins, ducking my slap. His friend comes over and removes Antonio's hand from my arm.

"Eh, Madonna! We would not hurt you! *Amici*—we are friends. *Vieni*, Madonna! You are safe with us. Here, would you like to ride this gentle animal? It is unseemly to make a *bella donna* walk such a distance. Allow me. . . ."

The first guy cups his hands and motions me to step up.

I hesitate: These guys look smarmy. But no stranger than any-thing else I've encountered in this unlikely voyage. And I'm sooo tired. "Well . . . it is kinda farther than I thought. . . ."

I step into the cup of his hands with my good foot, shoving the length of cape out of my way. When I realize using this foot would put me onto the mule facing backward, I pause to test whether my gimp ankle will support my weight. Then, out of the corner of my eye, I see a glint of metal flashing in the starlight: Antonio has a knife. He grabs Leo's cape—and my backpack along with it.

Cutpurses and thieves! With a sudden rush of adrenaline, I swerve and kick the knife out of his hand. He yells, cursing at me loudly, while his friend stops to pick up the knife. I only have a second to save myself. Grabbing my pack, I make a dash for dear life, mindless of my ankle. Even as I'm running, I manage to strap the backpack to my stomach and refasten Leo's cape around my shoulders.

I hear a donkey bray and one of the men panting in close pursuit. I have to lose them! I head for a grove of trees on the bank of the river, with no idea where I'm headed, except away from Antonio and his evil friend. At that moment, I notice a band of what must be gypsy families walking or pulling carts, carrying torches, and headed caravan-style across the bridge.

Not seeing an alternative, I scream at the top of my lungs, "HELP! RAPE!!! *Carnale!*"

A woman shrieks and grabs her child close for safety. Two men, colorfully dressed and carrying sacks on long poles, peel off from the gypsy band to charge at the cutpurses with their sticks.

Like a cloud of locusts, the women and children begin swarming around me, closing ranks as the men run in pursuit of the *banditos*. Their nearness, carrying along with them strange noises and smells, makes it difficult for me to breathe.

"Stop!" I shout, kicking, weaving, and ducking beneath arms attempting to grab and snatch at me, my hair, my cape.

I wrap the cloak tighter, looking for a way to escape the crush of the crowd, and run as fast as I can across the wooden bridge to continue on the path that runs parallel to the Arno on the other side. I pray it's the one that will take me into town. Now the path is narrow, and stepping off it might mean slipping down the steep banks into the cold, coursing river.

I slow my steps to avoid disaster. After what seems like an eternity—in the way that finding your way in a strange place without landmarks or, let's face it, GPS, always seems never-ending—I begin to see signs of life.

A quick look around: The veil of night is brightening and I begin to gain my bearings. This, finally, starts to look like the iconic postcard images of Florence I remember from home. Funny that I've wanted to visit here my whole life, and, as luck would have it, by the time I make it to Florence it's in a whole other century. While I am happy to be here, I wonder what it would be like to visit in my century, with my parents. And come to think of Gwen and Jerry, are they even aware that I've disappeared?

Homesickness fills my heart as I remember my mother is also in Italy, playing violin on a concert tour with the National Symphony Orchestra—almost near, and, at the same time, oh so far away!

I swallow past the lump in my throat. I stop to catch my breath, then slide to the ground, carefully stretching out the smelly, rag-bandaged leg to protect my bad foot.

The picture-perfect landscape of Florence blurs beneath my tears. Feeling sorry for myself is not going to help anything; meeting Leonardo is a dream come true. I am here to find out the secrets of his incredible mastery of art, engineering, science, invention—in short, everything under the sun. And if there's anything Gwendolyn Morton taught me, it's this: What I can dream, I can do.

I wipe my eyes with Leonardo's cloak, overly large and falling off my shoulders. I move forward, inspired.

Finally, I come upon a building with a large doorway, a public house. I enter the courtyard. There is a simple wooden sign over the tavern door in Italian: PER CHI DESIDERA TRATTENERSI E ESSERE ALLEGRI. I know from music that *allegri* means joyful, so I can't imagine it says anything bad. I also notice steps and a ramp that lead to the upper level, undoubtedly Leonardo's studio. I pound on the door, yelling breathlessly, "Someone! Anyone? Is Vincenzo there? Kairos sent me! I am his American—er, English—*cugina*."

A set of eyes peers out from behind a peephole in the door, grunting something incomprehensible. It's then I realize I am no longer wearing Translator. Did it fall off when I was fleeing those awful bandits? I can't have lost my only means of communication!

The woman hisses, *"Shh, regazza! Vi sveglierete le protezioni de' Medici!"* De' Medici. It's the only word I can grab on to. The ruler of Florence is Leonardo's patron, a man of enlightenment. Yet this woman seems afraid.

"I need to find Signora Vincenzo!" I sob. "Please. I mean *grazie*! Um, err, *prego*?"

I feel my lips begin to quiver and a sob escapes. At that, the woman cracks the door a tad wider, curious to get a closer look; flickering candlelight throws wild shadows against the wall.

"Leonardo *dice* . . ."

As if I've uttered a magic word, I hear the jingle of skeleton keys followed by the click of door bolts. A wizened red face framed by a white cap and wisps of graying hair peeks out guardedly.

"Io sono la Signora Vincenzo," she says.

"Oh, thank God!" I say, and grab her hand still holding the keys.

Still, she will only open the door enough to look me up and down.

I brush off the hood with my free hand and quick pull my hair out of its ponytail so it falls around my shoulders. It's then I feel something weighing down my hood. Translator! I put on the headphones and fluff my curls around them to mask the purple muffs, something that would undoubtedly raise suspicion. For once, I am happy to have big hair.

"Why, you're a tiny thing, aren't you? What are you doing out *di prima mattina?*"

I breathe a sigh of relief: The translation into English is coming through. I pray that Translator is working in both directions.

"Those thieves—they tried to steal my backpack and I ran, but they had a donkey and they're probably coming for me. And I'm starving! Maestro Leonardo said—" Feeling desperate, I grab her hand again. "Oh, please do let me in!"

As she pulls her hand from my grip, she says, "Oh, come now. This is not the face of *una brava. Come ti chiami?*"

"Charley. I mean, Carlotta. As soon as Kairos gets here—" Uttering Kairos's name earns a look of disapproval.

"Carlotta. You're a wild-looking thing. Kairos, you say? That boy is always finding wayward wenches. No matter, his heart is in the right place. Now, it is three florins a night for a bed." She holds her hand out with a frown, stubbornly blocking the door. "Payment in advance."

"Pay? A bed? Geez, I mean . . . I'm not going to sleep here or anything. But I hadn't thought . . . where . . . ?"

I begin weeding through the front pocket of my backpack for spare change, praying to heaven that something resembling currency might be tucked away. I spent most of my last allowance on supplies. I dig up a few pennies and my lucky Susan B. Anthony dollar. In the process, out spill random colored Post-its, paper clips, energy bar wrappers, aluminum foil, and ballpoint pens. A colorful braid of gummy worms, moistened by horse slobber so that they are now fused into one solid, squiggly snake, falls to the sooty ground at my feet. Ruefully, I think, there goes my quick comfort food.

"No, no, NO!" I am startled at her sudden screams and look up to see a terrified look cross Signora Vincenzo's face. "Who are you any-way, young daughter of Eve, carrying snakes that fall from your sack? *Strega!*" She kicks up the dust as if to bury the snake but then realizes it is not alive.

I bend to pick it up, dusting off the sticky thing and pretending to chomp down. "No, it's just candy. Or was. You know, sweets?" I say, frowning. Seeing the inert sugary mess in my hands, she leans in closer, then frowns.

"Si tratta di uno scherzo?"

"No, not a joke . . . and unfortunately, I don't have any euros. I should've asked my mom before she left for Flor—I mean, before I left home. Would you take a Susie B.?" I reveal the bright silver coin in my palm. "Or maybe you take credit? We get cash back. . . ." I flash my American Express card—per Jerry Morton, for emergencies only, and if this isn't an emergency, I don't know what is—before realizing, once again, there is no America, no credit card industry, no Dad. Not here.

"No, Madonna, I do not give credit to strangers," she sniffs, arms folded across her chest. "We are cheated by too many of the likes of you!"

"I'm good for it. I swear! Please, take the money. It's all I have right now, but I promise, I'll figure out how to get you more." I have no idea how this might actually happen, but I need to go inside and sit down. Get off my sore foot, at least.

Signora Vincenzo ponders this momentarily, then takes the

Susie B., holding it up to the light. Placing the coin between her teeth, she bites.

So many germs, I want to warn her. Doesn't she realize where that's been? But no, of course she doesn't. I see a greedy look dawning on her face.

"*Si. Viene*, Carlotta. You are English?"

"*Si, o no.* Well, it's sort of *difficile da* explain. I was in the garage showing Lexy the thingy, and he tried to kiss me. . . ." I pucker my lips. "Ugh! Then somehow, I must've bumped up against something that switched the machine on, but it was an accident, and suddenly, I was spinning . . . and Lex was gone!" I can't stop spewing.

"But then here I was . . . er, am . . . and there he was. Leonardo, that is. Firing cannonballs! He said I had to come here or Lorenzo would arrest me, but I need to talk to Leonardo some more and I can't go to prison!"

Signora Vincenzo looks perplexed. She lets out a long sigh of frustration.

"*In veritas,*" I try. "I won't rob you or anything," I promise, holding up three fingers in the Girl Scout pledge. I hope she recognizes "I swear" as some sort of universal signal. "And Leonardo is also expecting me." I feel my lip start to quiver again.

"And really, my foot—I twisted it. And this bruise . . ." I pull up the cape to show her. My ankle's blue, and swollen to baseball-size now. "Ser Leonardo sent Kairos to get something to calm the swelling. Could I sit down?" I pantomime sitting, to make sure she *capisce.*

This whole conversation isn't going well. It seems we are lost in translation, technology or no. I put my hands to my ears just in case Translator has fallen off again, and am only slightly reassured to feel the fur.

"You know, inside, maybe?" I'm starting to get a headache now, too.

Whether from the bump on the noggin or the long trip, I can't tell for sure. But I do know that if I have to stand up much longer, I might faint.

"Enter, Signorina," she commands after a long pause. "Then you aren't one of those *pazzi* girls? They're chasing Kairos day and night. They always land at *mia porta.*"

One of those crazy girls. Kairos is as bad as Lex, it would seem.

III.

People Will Be People!

I am ensconced in the tavern below Leonardo's studio where Signora Vincenzo, by all definitions the boss of the place, offered a horse trough and a rough cloth for bathing, a long dress made out of coarse brown wool—definitely not my style—and a beribboned cap to tamp down my wayward curls. Not sure I look a whole lot better after washing, what with the getup and this big bruise around my eye.

Meanwhile, the *donna* and her daughters have been up baking bread for at least two hours already, even though the rosy red fingers of dawn and all that Homer poetic stuff have barely scratched open the night sky. The girls, dressed much the same as me, are giggling and gossiping, except for the one in the middle, a girl around my age, who looks sullen. Typical teenager! Some really wasted dudes, who should have gone home hours ago, are snoring under tables.

I go outside, where the light of day hurts my eyes. Note to future self: sunglasses! But I thank goodness for that sun, as it is essential for keeping my devices charged.

I glance around what looks to be a barnyard, right in the heart of Florence. Horses tethered to posts near a stone wall. A musty stone stable that definitely could use a mucking. Chickens clucking and pecking in the courtyard. The bray of a donkey in the distance. And towels and sheets strung up on a line, flapping in a steady breeze. I shudder, remembering that I read about how places like this became breeding grounds for the spread of disease and plagues like the Black Death.

I figure out how to set up my solar battery for optimal sun and I think, I *pray*, the tablet will start charging. Again, I notice the hourglass replacing the normal hour-minute-second ticking of time. The sand is equally distributed, top and bottom. Does that mean it's been only a half-hour since I got here?

I carefully set the tablet at an angle on the stone fence and prop it against the barn. The battery looks like it's catching energizing rays. I stare at the tablet's screen and hold my breath. . . . YES! The battery icon thing shows it's charging, and I feel encouraged. It can charge, but it will probs happen R-E-A-L-L-Y S-L-O-W-L-Y, because some clouds are rolling in. At this rate, it may take five hundred years to charge up fully.

While it's charging, I might as well try to type up my notes on time travel for Billy, but I won't have much time before my absence inside the *taverna* will be noted. I fold my knees under me and, using the fence as a desk, pull the spiral out of my backpack. I flip quickly to where my notes end and, mindful that this might slow the charging, nervously begin to type.

While I'm pretty much 100 percent sure Billy wouldn't breathe a word of this to anyone, I feel compelled to encrypt a cautionary message that I'm hoping would pop up before anyone could read the post itself.

Blog Entry #1. FYEO

Space-Time Dimension (STD): @ today minus a bunch of centuries, the Republic of Florence

Spoiler alert: Mom and Dad, historians, archeologists, or whoever, if you are opening this blog prior to the year 2018, please read no further! And anyone in the FBI or CIA who may get a hold of this, redact all classified information about Operation Firenze, the Qualia Rosetta, or how I got myself into hot water here for telling the truth, as this information may change history. Or the future. Or a time-space dimension I am not yet aware of.

NEWS FLASH: IT WORKS! WE HAVE SUCCESSFULLY HACKED THE SPACE TIME CONTINUUM. I know you won't believe me . . . I find it hard to believe myself! But I swear, Billy, somehow that little frame model you superglued, the golden ratio, and Kairos's algorithm all came together in one split moment to break the time barrier.

I would send you a postcard to prove it, but Gutenberg's not yet in business and it is centuries before Louis Daguerre will invent the first real camera. Lucky for me, I have one on my phone! And I fear no one is aware of the outcome of the voyage of one New World explorer. In fact, I hardly know what's going on here myself; after all, it isn't like I can turn on CNN.

Because I am sure no one but you could possibly believe the reality of this discovery, I've marked this FYEO—For Your Eyes Only.

This is the first time I've had a chance to breathe. Literally. I mean, you try spiraling back in time half a millennium and let me know how you feel!

Anyway. Here goes our experiment in space-time blog transmissions. Luckily, I have my tablet. Must figure out if there's any weak signal of satellite transmission echoing in time to post this online and pray it gets to you.

By now, you may have heard that things with Lex in the garage didn't go so well. I have no idea how it happened, but

first, I was showing him one thing, and next I know, I'm plop-
ping down in an empty field in the black of night. Empty, that
is, until this crazed guy with a mane as wild as mine shows
up out of nowhere, covered with a hoodie and cloak, waving
his arms like a madman and cursing his fortune, in Italian
as it turns out. And you will never believe who the madman
turned out to be!

Leonardo: the very guy I came to see. He asked what I, a
mere girl, was doing out alone at midnight. A mere girl. And
people say I have an attitude!

Of course, I have a million questions for the great, the
magnificent, the Renaissance genius Leonardo da Vinci. . . .

Wow. Stay tuned, Billy, 'cause we're in the zone now!

Your Partner in Time Travel,

Charley

P.S. I am praying you receive this transmission and can
ping me back.

"Phew!" I breathe a sigh of relief as I hit send. Just then, a rooster jumps up and wanders over, probably attracted by the light. I see his reflection in the glare of the screen. "Don't even think about it!" I admonish him out loud. "Anyways, that's not a chicken, that's you, birdie boy-o." Last thing I need is a rooster doing a mating dance with his likeness on a tablet.

Evidently, I'll need to keep the tablet safe from rooster mating rituals—or any prying eyes from the House of Vincenzo. I pull the cape from around my shoulders and drape it artfully over the front of the tablet to block out the light—and the rooster's reflection—while keeping enough of the battery exposed to keep the charge going. I check the icon one more time to make sure. Still charging, thank the heavens.

Speaking of which, I notice the sun has risen significantly higher in those heavens. My tummy has begun to rumble again. I glance back in the direction I came from before dawn, wondering when Leonardo might appear. Signora Vincenzo and her daughters will undoubtedly be cooking up some luscious pasta for their customers, and maybe they'll be kind enough to let me scarf down leftovers—in exchange for pitching in on the cleanup. It's the least I can offer.

The dark *taverna* is lit only by an open hearth and a few smoky candles. The small, dirty windows let in little light and no air. It's smoky and stuffy. I smell bread baking, and the aroma makes my poor tummy growl. I discreetly nibble on an energy bar.

I fish out my science spiral and a pencil from my backpack to clear my head. I hope to be able to one day add these words into my Dear Diary at home—with nothing more technological than a mechanical pencil. And if my tablet keeps charging, I'll type up another blog for Billy—I need to tell him more about where I am and how different everything is in this godforsaken place. Although I gather from the gossiping women that it may be that God is a little too present here, in the form of a Dominican friar named Girolamo Savonarola (pronounced *jee-RAW-lah-maw sah-vaw-nah-RAW-lah*). If there's any chance under the Tuscan sun that my message reaches Billy, I want to ask him to send me a little internet research on the dude. 'Cause I'm guessing the only webs here are made by spiders.

In the meantime, Billy's gonna be shocked that the tavern owner is named Vincenzo! Same last name as his! Wonder, could Billy possibly be a descendant? I'll have to ask him how far back he can trace his family tree. Can you imagine if they were related? Too bad I didn't pack a swab to bring back for DNA testing.

I see Signora Vincenzo is rolling out dough on a long wooden table. I have to admit, if I'm gonna be stuck in fifteenth-century Italy, I might as well take advantage of the cultural experience. "Can I watch you make spaghetti?" I ask. My tummy's rumbling louder now, just thinking about original Italian home cooking.

"*Questo?*" She draws her eyebrows together in a frown like she has no idea what I'm talking about.

"Spaghetti! You know, pasta!" The daughters exchange comments, their hands raised to cover their mouths, which makes me mad, because it feels like the lunchroom at school when everyone's talking behind everyone else's backs and pretending no one will notice. "Pasta!" I repeat, getting more and more frustrated. "Spa-ghet-ti!"

"*Questo spa-ghet-ti?*" she repeats.

Maybe Translator's on the fritz. So I stretch out my arms and point at the dough—like, you know, roll it out long and thin. No recognition whatsoever. Finally, I spy a broom in the corner, and pull out a straw to show what spaghetti looks like and roll a bit of the dough up to resemble that. At that point, any pretense of being polite to a guest goes out the window; la Vincenza's daughters are all rolling on the floor laughing!

I'm about to cry again, until Signora Vincenzo goes to a shelf and pulls down a glass jar filled with macaroni noodles. "*Pasta,* Carlotta."

And I'm like, how come they don't get it? "Spaghetti, the official *cucina Italiana,* no?"

But what if I could actually show them what I'm talking about? I remember that last week I downloaded recipes from The Food Network thinking my mom and I would try out the electric pasta maker I gave her last Mother's Day. So I dash back to the courtyard where I've "plugged in" my tablet—luckily, it's about 85 percent charged—and run in to show them photos, ingredients and everything. If spaghetti isn't yet pasta, well then, I'll have to invent it.

They gather in a gaggle around me with screams and gasps, pointing fingers first at me, then at the tablet.

"Questo?"

"È la magia?"

"Esso's il diavolo!"

One girl, clearly freaking out, pulls out what I recognize to be my Susie B. coin and shoves it in my face, shouting, *"Questa ragazza è una strega!"*

I slap her hand away. "There is no devil and I am not a witch," I insist, although I'm realizing that showing them the tablet may have opened up a Pandora's box.

"No. It's just a picture. *Una tavoletta.* See?" I point to the picture on the screen. "Spaghetti. T-O-M-A-T-O. *Pomodoro.*"

I pantomime biting into an imaginary tomato and exclaiming over the taste, wiping my chin of its imaginary juices, to show them this is also food. My tummy grumbles.

Now the girls are going gaga. *"Pomodoro? Es rosso!"* exclaims the youngest, who looks about eight. *"Come un peperone!"* suggests her sister. Even the sullen one suddenly looks interested. *"O una mela,"* she concludes.

Red like a pepper? Or an apple? You'd think they'd never seen a tomato.

My mind is flashing back—or maybe it's forward. I'm trying to pull something out of my brain, which, besides traveling five hundred years across six time zones, has been running for twenty-four hours straight if anybody's counting. Not to mention, I took a good whack to the noggin.

Then it dawns on me—when Kairos returns with whatever might pass these days for a doctor, I need to double-check what year we're in. If I am where—or when—I think I am, there is no America on any European map. Irreverently, parts of a little poem that we learned in grade school pop into my head. "In fourteen hundred ninety-two, Columbus sailed the ocean blue. . . ."

But here in the actual fourteen hundred and ninety-two, on Europe's side of the ocean blue, the prospects for my mission to teach these particular Italians about their once and future culinary concoctions are somewhat less hopeful. Because it's likely too soon for news of Columbus's discovery to have reached these shores. And because, as I learned on my last visit to the American Indian Museum, the tomato is a New World fruit . . . that has yet to be discovered!

No wonder they're laughing at me.

IV.
Time Travel Is So Draining

It's all too much. I burst into tears and hobble back out to the court-yard, but there is no room to be alone with my humiliation. My ankle has swollen as big as the tomato that no one's ever seen before, and it's all I can do to stumble around.

The sun is rising, and people are milling about—coming in to eat after doing the early morning jobs of feeding chickens and horses or whatever it is they do here, or leaving, perhaps to get to the market. Townspeople passing by all seem to wash from the same trough in front of Vincenzo's.

Where else can I go? I shove the tablet and battery into my back-pack. Sick of the hot coverings muffling my ears, I surreptitiously pull the headphones off and stow them with the tablet.

I look again at the long ramp leading up to Leonardo's studio. There is no railing, though, and I am feeling too achy and weak to climb it. I spy what looks to be a stable and go inside. Although there are no an-imals, it appears to have been recently cleaned, because the stalls look swept and there's a mound of fresh straw by the door.

I plop down on the straw, not even caring what bugs may be hiding there. In my imagination, that hay bale was going to feel better than it did. Instead there are little pieces of hay poking at me all over, and the smell of manure and hot straw is a lot stronger than I'd noticed at first. But I am way too tired and sore to care, much less get up. After a long moment, I peel off my cap, wrap it around my swelling ankle, and use the ribbons to tie it. Then I kick a little bit of hay into a second pile, trying as best I can to elevate it a bit to slow the swelling. Where is ice when you need it?

I edge up enough to peer out a barred window. None of the girls have emerged from Vincenzo's, nor has the signora herself seen fit to check on me. For the moment, I am alone.

Thank goodness.

I fall back on the straw and allow myself a long, semi-blissful moment of pain-infused serenity. It is all so strange: One moment, I am at home speculating on the possibility of time travel; the next, I am in such a totally alien world. How can these times be running simultaneously?

Billy is probably the only other person in the universe who would think such thoughts with me. If only he were here, I would not feel so alone!

I pull out my tablet—it's holding its charge so far. Do I dare try to communicate with that other world? How much time has passed? Will anyone at home be wondering where I am? I must try again to reach Billy—Instagram? Too short. Snapchat? It disappears. Blog again? If there is an echo of molecular signals, a bounce that acts on the reverse time-space potential of the neutrino . . .

Blog Entry #2. FYEO

Space-Time Dimension (STD): @ today minus 511 years,
the Republic of Florence

Hey, again, Billy. Hoping you are getting these transmissions. It would be really super amazing to hear back from you. I am learning a few things here, none of which has anything to do with anything remotely civilized. They have me bathing in the horse trough. I am currently hiding inside a barn outside a tavern that may belong to some Vincenzo ancestor of yours.

I'm nursing a bum foot and had a good solid bump on the noggin upon landing (note to self for time-travel trip home: maybe a helmet?). Leonardo sent me back to his studio by myself and I was almost kidnapped along the way. Now I don't know where he is, but Kairos is supposed to come back here with a doctor to see if anything's broken. Yes, that *Kairos!*

I just made a fool out of myself with the signora of the family and her daughters by asking for spaghetti. Not yet discovered, apparently! And forget the tomato—that lovely fruit is completely undiscovered on this side of the millennium. And I'm so hungry!

My goal for now is simply to avoid becoming the laughing stock of Florence. La Vincenza's teenaged daughters act like Beth on steroids. Hard to keep your chin up when all you really want to do is cry.

But I'm not complaining! Just a little homesick, I guess. For all I know, I am in an alternate universe where Columbus has fallen off the edge and never reaches the New World. Meaning, goodbye, Charley!

Is this a message in a bottle, or can information flow forward in time? Good research question. Get back to me on that, okay?!

Your PITT,

Charley

V.

They Call It Macaroni

I must have been dozing. A clatter of hooves thunders in my ears, and I burrow deeper into the straw to avoid detection while slipping on Translator.

"Carlotta? *Dove tu?*"

Kairos. Before I can hop up to standing, his voice tapers off in the direction of the *taverna*. Then I hear Signora Vincenzo yelling at Kairos—"*Chi è,* Carlotta?! How could you invite her into our midst? *Lei è una strega!*"

She must be pointing Kairos in the direction I disappeared during my earlier humiliation because the voices are getting nearer. I freeze beneath my straw hideaway, but Kairos's horse is hot on my scent, and with one eye at the stable window, he snorts. It's the sugar: one lone, leftover gummy worm stuck to my earbuds. Just enough to lure one sweet-toothed horsey!

"Carlotta?" Kairos shoves the horse's rump out of the way and shades his eyes against the bars. I've apparently not hidden myself as well as I thought. "Ah, here she is, *la bella* Carlotta!" He laughs.

Then, speaking to Signora Vincenzo, he says, "She is quite clever, this girl. But she is no witch! *Mia cugina* loves *la commedia dell'arte,* you see!"

At this, I feel obliged to sit up. Thank goodness for the dim light; no one can see my burning face.

Signora Vincenzo can't let it go. "*Questo pomodoro*, Kairos? Carlotta begged me to make her '*spaghetti Pomodoro.*'"

"*Si, es delicioso!*" Kairos is acting as if this is a perfectly natural conversation. "An English delicacy. You should try it, Signora. And her peanut butter and jelly sandwiches . . ." He kisses his fingers and opens the door. I squint at the light coming in. It must be late morning.

"Anyway, there's been a slight change of plans, Carlotta. The Maestro was delayed, so if Leonardo can't get here to you, we must get you to Leonardo."

"Huh?" I stammer inarticulately (meaning I am at a loss for words!). "I thought Ser Leonardo was coming here."

Kairos winks, then swings the stable door wide, offering me a hand up. I try not to wince with the weight on my foot.

Signora Vincenzo clucks like one of the hens roaming the yard.

"*Scusi*, Signora!" Kairos pulls me by the hand. I narrowly avoid stumbling into La Vincenza. "But Leonardo awaits!"

She seems to finally get the message, starting reluctantly back toward her kitchen.

Kairos lends me a shoulder as I hop outside. "*Bellissima!*" he laughs, brushing the straw from my hair.

"Bedraggled is more like it." I push back my hair, now feathered with hay, and try to take stock of my physical state.

I'm a mess. I pull straw from my head, then realize I am like a scarecrow from head to foot. I begin to brush other stable scraps from my leggings and notice how I'm already wearing holes in the soles of my ballet flats. Pointlessly, I wonder if there's a place I could buy more appropriate shoes. Me, who's broke. Maybe I could trade up for a solid pair of work boots.

"You look fine, Carlotta," Kairos remarks, eyeing me critically up and down. "Just like a stable boy."

"Ha! Stable boy! Guessing girls don't get that job?!" I say sarcastically, shifting my weight to my good foot.

He shakes his head, as if this were common knowledge.

"Figures," I say mockingly. "Anyway, first things first: What did the doctor say? I could use acetaminophen—for pain if not swelling."

"No, Signorina, I am afraid we have no pills here. To calm the black and blue around your eye, the apothecary has mixed you an ointment of chamomile, witch hazel, and aloe vera. You are familiar with these remedies?"

I nod. Kairos is looking more serious now. He pulls a long linen bandage from the pouch over his horse's back. "He recommends you apply the same to your foot. After that, his prescription is for rest. There's nothing else he can do."

"Hmmph. Sounds like one of my mom's homeopathic remedies." I feel a sudden deep longing: If only Mamma were here!

I plop back down as Kairos, chuckling, takes my ankle. "Think of me as a substitute for *tua mamma*. Does that hurt?" His touch is surprisingly gentle. He takes off my shoe and, removing Leonardo's oily rag, carefully begins to wrap a clean linen cloth around my leg and foot.

"Where'd you learn to do that?" I ask.

"Being Leonardo's apprentice, one learns about many things. One is anatomy; another is that one must treat the human form with reverence. And, you might say, I bring other perspectives as well."

So cryptic! But I welcome his healing touch. The support of the bandage eases the throbbing. I attempt to stuff my foot back into my little ballet shoe; too swollen. Kairos takes my hand to pull me up, but I can't support my weight and almost fall face first. He tries to right me, but I'm so wobbly, I sink back down in a sprawl. I suddenly feel discouraged.

"Stay strong! I believe you have much to accomplish in your time here in Firenze, Carlotta. Can you ride a horse?" he asks.

I try to rally my spirits to meet his. "Can I ever!" I exclaim with effort, even though most of my riding experience is of the merry-go-round variety.

Kairos's mount is standing by the trough taking a long, sloppy drink of water. "Ew, that is gross!" I say. "You dirty old thing—what did I just wash in!"

The horse neighs and Kairos gives me a smirk. "He's cleaner than you are!"

I sigh. It's probably true.

"Carlotta, you must not delay. The Maestro awaits."

I feel a surge of energy. "Yes, I can do this! I came here on a mission; I cannot give up now. And then Leonardo can help me figure out how to get home, right?"

Kairos leans down and, taking my hand, pulls my arm across his shoulder, helping me hop toward the horse.

"Ser Leonardo says you hold the key," Kairos says with an awkward stare.

"The key!" Does the golden compass unlock the door to time—future as well as past? I pray it's still in my backpack. "Didn't you give me that key, Kairos?"

"I am only the apprentice, Carlotta. My master trusts you have the tools to unravel time's mystery at its heart."

I recall the strange markings etched into the golden compass and wonder again what they might signify. I hop quicker as Kairos practically throws me up onto the horse, then leaps up behind me.

"Does this horse have a name, Kairos?"

"*Uno nomme?* He flies, swift as winged Mercury." Kairos drops the reins around my body, clucking encouragingly. Mercury, taking a few skittish steps backward, is in no hurry, it seems.

"At this pace, he's less like Mercury," I say, tummy grumbling again, "and more like Macaroni!"

"Maccheroni!" Kairos bursts out in laughter as he kicks Macaroni into high gear. I grab on to Kairos as the horse rears up, and realize that this horseback riding business—bareback, no less!—is not going to be as easy as I thought.

"*Si*, Maccheroni it is, then. Carlotta, *mi fate ridere!* I am sure Leonardo will find humor as well as learning in your company. He awaits you at the church of that heretic, Savonarola. *Andiamo*, Maccheroni!" he shouts, as the mercurial Macaroni flies like the wind, and, from my high perch, I get my first real daylight glimpses of Florence.

As we bump along on horseback, it's like being inside a dream. And if it is a dream, it's the craziest, smelliest, noisiest, bumpiest, and most jarringly real dream ever. Here I am in Florence, Italy, in the wrong century. I marvel as we ride through the stone, mortar, and sand-paved streets and alleys that have stood since Roman times; who am I to be experiencing this miracle out of time, in the cradle of the Renaissance?

I feel so insignificant.

We burst out of the alley at a fast trot, skirting around the perimeter of what appears to be the central marketplace.

"Is Florence always this bustling with crowds?" I ask Kairos.

Before he can answer, I hear this weird *"woo-woo-woo!"* Sounds like an alien spaceship blowing its horn.

Macaroni startles and stops so short that I feel myself sliding off the horse's back.

"What the heck?" I ask, tightening my arms around Kairos to avoid falling off. Without looking up, I can only glean the shadow of something rather large speeding across our path.

Macaroni rears, then begins to sidle and snort.

"*Calmo, destri fidati!*" Kairos tightens up on the reins.

I am far from calm. My heart is racing—a feeling reminiscent of the all too recent clothes dryer churning of my ride through time. "No, seriously, that thing just now, Kairos—what was it?"

Kairos reaches forward to stroke Macaroni's neck and almost throws me over his head in the process. "Never fear, Carlotta. It is but an ostrich."

As if to prove he's real, the ostrich comes circling back in front of us, puffing up its neck to once again issue its deep-throated "*woo-woo-woo.*" The bird—which has to be over eight feet tall, what with that long neck—is kind of like the Road Runner in the cartoons, I think, until I look up over Macaroni's and Kairos's heads: I see the giant creature open first one wing, then the other in a choreographed little ostrich dance, after which it squats down, still flapping, and kicks out its legs. It is clearly meant as a warning: Don't mess with the bird.

"You're kidding me. An ostrich!"

Kairos continues clucking and whispering sweet nothings in Macaroni's ear.

"I cannot understand your insistence that I am a goat, Carlotta, but no. (This is a reference to how we met—I asked if he was "kidding" me during Take Your Child to Work Day at my dad's office, and he took me literally. But that was many lifetimes ago.)

When I don't respond, Kairos turns his head, looking at me expectantly. I nod, so he will go on.

"The wealthy families keep many exotic animals in their walled gardens—a small zoo, you might say. But normally, these birds do not escape, for they cannot fly."

"Ostriches." I repeat myself, having a hard time grasping this big bird as a pet.

"Is that not what I said?" Kairos is sounding frustrated. "Here, these flightless birds are prized also for their large eggs. Surely you have eaten ostrich eggs?"

"Can't say that I have," I reply snarkily.

Another *woo-woo* grunt sets Macaroni skittering—and me slipping off his back.

"Hold on tight!" Kairos turns Macaroni's head sharply and digs in a heel to spur him out of the path of Big Bird.

Macaroni turns in a wide circle and begins to run, the ostrich now running behind us. "No! No!" I shriek, breathless. I tighten my arms around Kairos's neck, holding on for dear life until I can regain my seat, then look around to see him begin his little ostrich dance in front of some people trying to buy linens from a street vendor.

"Watch out, he's going to kick!" I shout.

"You must remain *calmo*, Carlotta. You will frighten it further and leave the market in chaos," Kairos warns in a low voice, gripping my hands with his own—at least the one not holding the reins. "Hold tight!"

Kairos makes a *woo-woo* imitation, evidently trying to distract the animal and keep it from attacking, pulling again on Macaroni's reins. The horse leaps ahead.

The ostrich pursues, its ungainly body making chase, while the merchants scramble to get out of the way, grabbing their goods from their stalls to keep the beast from destroying their livelihood. By now we have attracted the attention of a group of uniformed men on horseback—it occurs to me they must form part of *Magnifico*'s security detail—as they form a wide blockade. I notice some of the men closest to Big Bird unfurling coils of rodeo-like ropes.

"Don't hurt the poor beast!" I shout, fearing for the worst. I can hardly watch as they encircle the animal, shouting, taunting, and waving sticks and ropes—apparently in an all-out effort to capture—or kill—it.

Looking around, I notice we've stirred up quite the commotion, and I feel suddenly exposed. I am aware that my behavior must be calling attention to me, a mere girl, and not in a good way.

"Ca-ca-*Carlotta*," Kairos chokes out. "You must—*como se dice*—cool it. For your own sake, and the horse as well."

"But I can't let them hurt that poor thing, Kairos!"

"It is just an animal, Carlotta. They likely treat people who they suspect do not follow their customs no better." I take this as a warning.

Taking advantage of the distraction of the crowd, stirred up and watching the royal guard go into action against Big Bird, Kairos directs Macaroni to an alley leading into the square, where he settles the horse so we can set course again toward our destination.

"Redirecting," I say, doing my best GPS imitation.

"Let us not detour again, Carlotta," Kairos says. "Recall, you must keep your rendezvous with Ser Leonardo."

"Uh-huh," I blurt out, chastened by this latest adventure. Things just keep getting stranger and stranger. I must start to capture this for posterity. 'Cause, like, ostriches are the least of it now.

And even Billy wouldn't believe this scene.

As we make our way, far from that maddening crowd, I pull up a voice-recording app on my tablet, and in a shaky voice, I begin dictating an audio blog for the ages—or for Billy. Whatever comes first.

Blog Entry #3. For Your Eyes Only

Caro Billy,

Hope you're getting this. Lots of noise here. I have to be quick.

This place goes beyond your wildest imagination. Like, I'm riding on Macaroni, the horse, behind Kairos through the streets of Florence on our way to meet Leonardo at some church, when, for no obvious reason, he rears . . . because an ostrich just ran interference in front of Macaroni at a hundred miles an hour, stopped, and did a Big Bird version of kung fu karate. To say Macaroni was spooked . . .

As for me, I was hanging on for dear life!

Seriously, though. Can't help but wonder if maybe I'm recording this for posterity. Frankly, I'm scared. My electronics are my lifeline, but if they die . . . ? The solar battery helped a bit to recharge my tablet here, but it's SOOO slow. Doubtful it can ever store up enough juice to power myself back to the future from here. And if I'm stuck out of time, I imagine the shock when somebody someday excavates this time's earth layer to find remnants of Renaissance culture and digs up an "ancient" tablet. They're gonna make up some bogus story about the advanced technology of the fifteenth century. Little could they know!

But then, they'd also have to uncover what the real history of the Renaissance looks like. I mean, the Disneyfied version would have this looking like a civilized moment of high culture. But no! Picture the Arno River as a filthy bathtub, naked boys jumping in at dawn, while the women wade in knee deep in their dresses, scrubbing pots and chamber pots (is that the origin of "potty," I wonder?) in the same place! And humans and horses drinking from the same water trough. Gross.

But as Shakespeare might say, more anon. Wait—has Shakespeare been born yet?

Your partner in time travel,

Charley (a.k.a. Carlotta)

VI.

Burning Beauty

Kairos and I are approaching the famous Church of San Marco. I have managed to shove my bandaged foot back into my ballet flat to look respectable enough to enter this place of worship.

The approach to San Marco is impressive enough, but once Kairos helps me hop inside, I can't tear my eyes from the opulent murals, statues, and gilded icons that adorn the chapel with its massive dome. I could use sunglasses inside. 'Cause they really went crazy back then with the gold-leaf paint. And even though candlelight is the main illumination, the reflection hurts my eyes.

The pipe organ is topped with gilded angels. There's a priest standing behind the altar. He's thin and angry looking, but with a hypnotic voice that rings even to the back pews, where hundreds of worshippers listen with rapt attention. Kairos informs me the priest is none other than the golden-tongued Girolamo Savonarola, a Dominican friar who preaches against the evils of the material world. Allegedly, according to Kairos, Savonarola is famous for instigating the Bonfire of the Vanities. He urges the noble people of Florence to bring all their riches—art, furs, jewels, paintings, books, wigs, and other finery, stuff he preaches represents sins against the Almighty—into the main square of the city to be burned in a giant bonfire. Why anyone would burn books and paintings, priceless treasures of the actual Renaissance, is beyond me!

In fact, I can hear Savonarola preaching before we even enter the sanctuary. I pull Translator tight over my ears so I can understand his sermonizing.

"It would be good for religion if many books that seem useful were

destroyed. When there were not so many books and not so many arguments and disputes, religion grew more quickly than it has since."

I feel Savonarola's commanding presence. And he's making an impression! All kinds of people—noblemen and ladies, soldiers and guards, farmers and peasants, young and old—fill the pews, crying, praying. A few of the older men look bored. The ladies open fans to cover their mouths; I can almost hear the susurrus of whispers passing between them.

I guess this is all business-as-usual for pious Florentines.

"Jeez, I wonder what he'd think of *Harry Potter*," I say.

"*Silenzio*, Carlotta. This is a house of worship." Kairos hurries down the aisles, pulling me along, ignoring my snide remarks.

An eruption from the pulpit as Savonarola works his sermon up to a crescendo. "*Ecce gladius Domini super terram, cito et velociter.*" According to Translator that means "Behold the sword of the Lord will descend suddenly and quickly upon the earth."

I stop in my tracks. "Way harsh!" Kairos elbows me. Was I talking out loud? I hurry to clarify. "I mean, what in the world are they that could be so evil?"

"Carlotta, we are not here to judge. Remember, these are different times!"

Reprimanded, I tune in again to Translator. There's something familiar about this Savonarola guy's tone—like if he were living in my day, he'd have his own reality show. Mesmerizing but dangerous.

"*Vene, pronto*, Carlotta!" Kairos urges, pulling me again by the hand.

I can't help but stare. Most people are in the pews, but there's a crowd pressing ever closer to the pulpit. Savonarola seems to be a rock star, but the reaction of the growing mosh pit of fans—crying and beating on their chests—is like nothing I've ever seen.

"The Weepers," Kairos explains, cupping his hand to my ear to overcome the noise. "*Piagnoni*, they are called. They follow Savonarola everywhere."

Weepers! But what are they crying about?

We're veering off to one side of the church, nearly empty of worshippers and, thankfully, much quieter. As we get nearer, I spy Leonardo sitting quietly to one side, folio in hand, sketching details from the scene before him.

But the priest in the pulpit in front of us is apparently not finished with his sermonizing.

"The knowledge of things to come is a Divine prerogative, which, had the heathen gods been good spirits, they would not have claimed. For they did not, like our prophets, say, 'Thus saith God.' They spoke as of themselves, pretending to prescience of the future, and seducing men into superstition."

"So he's saying that no one can tell the future but God. Wow." I reflect on my own apparent powers of prophecy—and the "magic" tablet that proves that my future exists. "Wonder what he'd say if he knew I know the future—and that it's based on fact, not faith?"

"Hold your tongue, Carlotta. You had best keep that future to yourself if you wish to remain safe!" Kairos warns angrily. Seems he's still irritated with me for that whole detour in the marketplace.

"Should the good friar, or his Weepers, perchance learn of your tablet, he will not be so easily mollified. You must understand the power this so-called man of God holds among his followers: Fra Savonarola would destroy all that speaks to beauty, to knowledge, to the perfection of mankind. And he can whip his Weepers into a frenzy; they are drawn in to be spiritual warriors in his service."

Kairos casts a wary gaze at Leonardo, now turning to sketch the profile of an elderly man in the pew in front of us, rapt in attention at Savonarola's words. Leonardo seems unaffected by the commotion.

Kairos's admonishments seem no less directed at him. "Even the Maestro is not safe, should his works fall into the wrong hands."

"Nothing strengthens authority so much as silence," Leonardo scolds, shaking his head. "And many have made a trade of delusions and false miracles, deceiving the stupid multitude. Blinding ignorance does mislead us. O! Wretched mortals, open your eyes!"

"Maestro," Kairos interrupts him in a stage whisper, "here is Madonna. Be warned, though: She does not hold her tongue!"

"I have my rights, Kairos! I didn't come all this way to be told to shut up!"

"The greatest deception men suffer is from their own opinions," Leo mutters quietly.

"Yeah!" I can't help flinging back. "Like he says!" And I stick out my tongue at Kairos.

There is a momentary pause in Savonarola's preaching.

"I warn you to behave as befits a Renaissance maiden," Leonardo says, sounding for all the world like a certain former best friend. "You must contain your passions and only reveal yourself to those who would be friends."

I hate to admit it, but I'm kind of missing Beth, now that I think of it.

Kairos flashes a grin. "Yes. Friends, Carlotta?"

"*Amici*," I say, extending a fist.

Kairos returns the fist bump, but then turns serious. "And if I may, friend, a word of warning: Your magic slate, should it fall into the wrong hands, could prove exceedingly dangerous."

For the first time since tapping out a blog post to Billy, I think about the power of my tablet—and wonder how long that power will serve its purpose. The battery, though holding for now, is sure to drain. And then how will I access enough power to reverse engineer my time machine—the only magic that has any chance to point me back in time?

Back home. I pull the tablet from my backpack to be sure it's still here. Sure enough, the battery reads that it's holding its charge at 75 percent. A miracle, to be sure! I sigh with relief.

Leonardo says, "Remember, you have powerful tools at your fingertips, Carlotta. Your tablet . . . are there more mirrors of other worlds that you have carried here? These . . . objects . . . they have powers to connect you—and us—beyond today."

Leo has me searching my brain: "Mirrors of other worlds" with powers to connect us. Is the tablet my only power here? And what happens when the hourglass of power runs out?

My phone! I pat myself down, momentarily forgetting where I stowed it, trying to think about how to back up the tablet to my phone. I root through my backpack: Yes, it's in here.

"More than such 'modern' magic, you must see to it that the golden compass remains in your possession at all times, Carlotta," Kairos continues in a low voice. "More than your solar antenna or any modern invention, *this* key holds within it the power that you seek."

"What do you mean?" I ask. Although it clearly has its own magic, I have no idea how to access it.

I think back to how I got here in the first place. Billy placed only one of the two compass keys into our model structure, and that was enough to power our machine. That, and a kiss. I blush, feeling again the heat of Lex's lips.

I peer into my backpack again, this time for the golden compass. It's not in any of the pockets. I'm about to panic when I spy a dull glimmer: The golden compass is somehow locked into place in a corresponding groove sculpted into the Horse and Rider maquette. I am sure it wasn't there before.

Kairos bends down to show me how to remove it from the statuette, and his proximity again makes me blush. "Um, but how—?"

"Leave us!" Leonardo orders his apprentice. "There is work for you in the atelier."

Kairos bows ruefully and, without a word, exits.

Watching Kairos scurry out, I notice that the air is still filled with Fra Savonarola's inflammatory words.

Leonardo nods toward the fiery preacher. "Listen to the pious Dominican," he says. "But do not confuse words with wisdom. Savonarola has mastered words to manipulate the masses." He gestures to the worshippers sitting and kneeling in rows all around us. "You see, there are three classes of people: those who see, those who see when they are shown, and those who do not see."

"Yeah. I *so* get that," I mutter, thinking how nothing about human nature has changed with time. "I can think of a few blind people in my own time who don't see *me*, that's for sure."

As Savonarola holds up his hands in blessing, the crowd roars approval.

VII.
LEARNING FROM THE MASTER

"We must go."

I snap to attention as Leonardo puts away his folio and charcoal into a leather pouch affixed to his belt. He rises quickly, grabs my hand, and pushes through the crowd of parishioners, dragging me to the door.

"There are too many eyes and ears here. Kairos has told me, you come from a distant time and place, no? I must hear more about this *miraculoso viaggio*. Tell me about *A-mer-i-ca*. What scientific wonders does the future hold? These I must know!"

He wants to know! Again, I am struck at how our roles are reversed. I came here to learn from the great Renaissance genius, yet he is asking me all the questions. But like any great genius, I get that his hunger for knowledge is insatiable. (I love this word. It means "never satisfied." It's like when you can never get enough to eat. Like me, here, now.)

"What lessons can I possibly teach the Maestro?" I ask. And then I realize there's been a whole lot of new developments on Planet Earth—not to mention outer space—since then (since now?). The idea of filling the Master in on a half-millennium's worth of happenings is a little daunting.

But as Kairos just reminded me, I have more than one tool at hand to connect to the world. Just as Leonardo has his sketches and notes to capture the moment, I need to "sketch" notes, too. One person couldn't possibly explain everything that's happened everywhere, though. Hopefully, brainiac Billy will be able to chime in here. Fingers crossed, some fragment of my message gets through!

As the church bells toll the hour, Leonardo rushes me outside along the banks of the Arno River. What hour it is, I'm too tired to count. Although the salve Kairos applied to my ankle temporarily anesthetized the pain, I'm still hop-limping through a crowded, chaotic tangle of alleys and narrow streets. We dodge street urchins playing tag. Merchants push past, their carts heavily laden with cloth, spices, flowers, and fruit. A few noblemen walk by on their way to what Leonardo explains is the *Signoria*, sort of like our U.S. Congress but Renaissance Florence–style. I sure hope these guys get along better than the elected officials in Washington!

We weave through a maze of streets and piazzas—paved with cobblestones, irregular and slippery—that crop up and radiate out in a dizzying and nonsensical array, until I am completely lost. As if "lost" is unusual for me under the best of circumstances.

The air stinks to the high heavens. "A night of revelry," Leonardo explains, "leading up to Lent." As if that explains the ordure, the vomit, the single boot, and the empty tins that must've recently held spirits, judging from the stench. I wouldn't believe pollution could actually be worse before the advent of the factory, the car, coal-burning furnaces—but it seems to be so!

I hold my nose, trying not to be distracted from whatever wisdom Leonardo might impart. It seems he's got a lot on his mind.

" . . . and I have been impressed with the urgency of doing. Knowing is not enough; we must apply. Being willing is not enough; we must do."

"Right." It's like listening to a Shakespeare monologue. If there was a Shakespeare. Yet.

"I sense that you, Carlotta, have done what I have only *speculated* could be done. I have experimented with time . . . hence Kairos, my apprentice . . . but, then, you seem to have unlocked a mystery that is unknown in these days. You see, eternity is part of a vast continuum, related to the here and now. Not a line or a cube, but a . . . something vastly more intricate."

"Yep. Know exactly what you mean, Leo. Can I call you Leo? You guys are so formal here. But the form—a spiral! I'd swear I got here spiraling backward!"

To demonstrate, I stop and spin like a top. Suddenly dizzy, I stumble backward, forward, and stop in my tracks, arms spread for balance, feet planted in a widened stance.

"*L'uomo universale.*"

"*Exactemente,*" I reply, trying to give at least a partially accurate response in Italian, headphones or no. "Perspective. A universal principle, like the Fibonacci numbers. Your golden ratio! That's why, when Kairos gave me the golden compass, I had to show it was all part of one principle as part of my science project. But no one's been able to demonstrate that time travel is actually possible, much less how it might work—"

"This I have dreamt. Because I suppose the potential of reality to be limitless. With enough speed and force—ours is but a crude model. By chance, I found a target . . . *una donna della futura* whose advanced technology might bring this dream to us."

"Hmm—so my being here is all by chance?" I wonder at that. "At my dad's office, the computer was left on, directed to this moment in history . . . but light speed?" My mind is jumping ahead at light speed trying to take in the implications.

"Computer? There are ancient legends of machines calculating the movements of the heavens, but this is the stuff of myth. Yet now, you say, man is capable of computing light speed? This interests me. What, pray tell, is light speed?"

Still struggling to keep pace with Leonardo's long strides, I pull out my tablet, careful to keep it close under my cloak—no telling what *banditos* might be hanging about. Perhaps if I show him . . . But, of course—no internet!

I rush to explain anyway. "The speed of light has been determined as 30,000 kilometers per second."

"This, then, can be foretold by a computer?" Leonardo looks impressed. "And how fast is that, pray tell?"

I recognize that they don't even measure in minutes here, much less seconds. And distance seems to be an approximate thing. Is this what our world would be like if nothing were standardized, I wonder?

"Okay, so. Light speed is the time it takes light from the sun, or any star, really, to reach us over the distance between it and Earth—and nothing can travel faster than this, according to Einstein's relativity."

"*Eye-n-stein*. This is a star?"

Well, he was, back in the day. "A brilliant physicist."

It occurs to me that, during my voyage, I may have violated Einstein's proof. And any number of other so-called "laws" of physics.

"Say, Ser Leonardo, I am wondering . . . could I have somehow traveled faster than light . . . or . . . how do I know you're not making this all up? Or that I'm not dreaming?"

Suddenly, Leonardo stops, fully absorbed in an idea percolating inside his brain, and gesticulating madly at the busyness around us.

"Humbly, Madonna, until last midnight, I did not even know for sure *you* were possible. I know only that you arrived embracing the *modello* Kairos claims to have left for *future learning*, a guest in my 'now' on the banks of the Arno."

"Yes, well, as great as it is to be your guest, I am hoping to stay long enough to learn a few things up close and personal. You know, like how did someone with no formal schooling from a dysfunctional family grow up to be the great Maestro of all things? That kind of stuff," I say, mentally preparing to interview him. Interviews with experts can count up to 25 percent of the science fair score. I know I should be recording this on my phone, but I'm afraid of draining the battery even quicker, so I root through my backpack and pull out a purple gel pen—my signature writing piece—and my mini spiral notebook. The pen causes a raised eyebrow, and I realize that, back in the day, writing technology would be more like goose feathers and inkwells.

"Umm, maybe we could sit?" I motion to a stoop and pretend to sit. "The wrapping around my foot is coming loose, and I can't really write and walk at the same time, and, well, I was hoping to ask you a few questions about—"

But Leonardo interrupts again. "Yes, this above all else: to develop a complete mind, study the science of art, study the art of science. Learn how to see. Realize that everything connects to everything else."

I start jumping up and down with excitement. "Yes, er, *si*! *Parlo piu lento, prego*! Slow down here!" I say, scribbling as fast as my left hand can manage. "This is exactly what I am determined to show—how those discoveries and new ways of seeing in your day connect with science and technology advances in ours! Can you share your secret?"

"But *cara* Carlotta, it is *your* secrets that fascinate me! You know much that I can only dream about. You, and that magic slate of yours!"

"Yeah, well they've digitized everything in my day. All ones and zeroes in multiple algorithms. They say this is the future, so I'm learning to code: create patterns to reproduce books, music, even your art and inventions." I pause to check and see that Leo is getting this; he has that glint in his eye again. I pull up an e-book to demonstrate: *The World of Leonardo*. It's an old-fashioned art book my mom gave me in digital format. A treasure trove.

"See, here, for example, is your most famous painting, the *Mona Lisa*!"

"*Uno libro* made out of light!" says Leo, gazing at the screen, and then at me. "*Dio* has created this?"

I shake my head. "No, it's just a modern innovation on the printing press. Just another device to store printed books."

"*Incunabula*," he corrects me, using the Latin word for printed books in the 1400s. When he looks back, his eyes soften. "And who is this . . . Mona Lisa?" He reverently points to the image.

"Oh, yeah. *Mona Lisa* is what we call your most famous masterpiece—*la Giaconda*!"

"I know not of *una Giaconda*."

I clap my hand over my mouth and bite my tongue. "Oopsies, maybe I said too much." I scan the text and notice he wouldn't begin painting her until 1502.

"Ten years *alla futura*! *Eh, bene*! This is something I have to look forward to." He pulls out his sketch notes and a stick of charcoal, as if inspired.

"And you, Carlotta, may I sketch your portrait? There is something quite arresting in your face."

Arresting! It occurs to me that an authentic Leonardo sketch—of me, no less—would be a great addition to the science fair presentation. I mean, who would doubt my story if I had a personalized parchment to bring home!

"Perhaps you will, *como se dice, di-gi-tize* it here?" he taps on my tablet and inadvertently closes out the image of his own masterwork.

"Wow, wish I had thought to download a drawing app—you could create the first digitized portrait, Leo!" I giggle at the thought.

Then I see how little juice I have left in the battery. I am really gonna need to charge this baby good before long, or my "magic" will be kaput.

I pull the tablet back from Leonardo's hands, hoping to avoid a complete shutdown, but not before I hear the faintest echo of a familiar voice:

"I wish Charley had come, too. She would so love this."

Mamma!

VIII.
My Magical Mystery Tour

"Oh!" I feel my throat tighten as my heart skips. I wonder whether I'm imagining things, but from the newly curious look on Leonardo's face, he heard it, too.

"What voice emanates from the digits?" Leonardo seems to be concentrating on listening as much as seeing. He reaches for my tablet, winking. "Would I could see what my ears can hear!" he smiles. Leo's charm campaign doesn't feel all that different from Lex's earlier reason-disarming attempts.

"Nothing to see, Leo," I say, squeezing my fingers tighter around my tablet. "I think it's just a recording." Could be I accidentally hit play on one of my video interviews with the parentals for social studies. "You know. Oral family histories. It's so easy to do videos, you know—er, uh—"

"*Wi-DAY-o*—I see," Leonardo points out, helpfully translating from the Latin. "Then it is not just words and pictures on your *dee-WAES*?"

"Yeah, well, we can create moving pictures these days—not these days, but . . . you know. Anyway, sharing video is a lot quicker than the Pony Express."

"*Si*. The fastest horse. I will show you," Leonardo interrupts, pulling more scraps of paper out from his belt, quickly sketching, right in front of my eyes. First a line that turns into a rear haunch. Then the long oval of a snout. Angles for ears. And a flying mane. Cartoons, I think they called them then. Not like *The Simpsons*, or *Zits*, but quick sketches that later got incorporated into actual masterpieces. That someday, someone would pay a gazillion dollars for!

But it is a *miracolo* to see the Maestro in action. I can't help but cluck in wonder at the clean lines that emerge on the page of the sketch artist.

"Anyways, we don't travel by horse much anymore . . . and the internet, well, it's global, you see, and it's kinda well known that the *mobile telefono* isn't reliable without—"

"Global? *Questo . . . glo-bal?*"

Oops again. Five hundred years too soon to be talking about telephones and the like.

"Hey, Ser Leonardo, pray tell me: *Questo annos et mensa est?*"

"Why, it is *otto mars, 1492 Anno Domini.*"

March 8! Churning random factoids through my admittedly over-loaded mind, I draw one conclusion: If we don't celebrate Columbus Day until October, and we're in March of the same year Columbus makes landfall, the whole flat-Earth thing would be accepted fact in this time—a myth that must be well enforced by the powers that be.

Before I can think through the implications, I hear Mom's voice again. This time, there's no mistaking a taped interview for a live event. "Giuliana? *Ciao, ecco! Si* . . . I've just arrived. No, I couldn't convince Charley to join me this trip."

I quick sneak a peek at my screen. My mom is walking through an airport—is it Dulles, where the National Symphony Orchestra took off for their Italian concert tour? But the inside of the airport looks unfamiliar, and the signs are in Italian and English. It's like I'm operating in a parallel universe.

"Wait!" I blurt out to Leo in my confusion. "Do you have the time?" I point to my wrist. Immediately, I have to laugh at the joke time's playing on me. There's not yet a wristwatch to be seen in all of Firenze. And it might be a couple hundred years before time would be that portable. Daylight is probably life's default setting when candles and burning oil provide the only artificial light.

I tune in to the sounds around me to hear the chiming of church bells. The *Campanile* here, the main clock, is chiming the half-hour, which one, I don't have a clue. But if it is today, then I think Mamma's supposed to be arriving in Firenze about 8 a.m., local time.

I peek under the cover of my tablet to see her again.

There she is! Mom's carrying her priceless Amati violin—the one insured for millions by Lloyds of London and that is never out of her hands when she travels—like a baby. But I am her baby! I pace a few steps away from Leo, out of hearing range—I hope.

"Giuliana, *absolutamente*, we must get our girls together again soon!"

Judging from the convo, she's on video chat with her friend Giuliana, whose annoying daughter Carolina is a violin prodigy. A real one.

"Maybe this summer. I know she will come, if only for the pasta and the chance to play history detective. You know my daughter: obsessed with spaghetti and all things da Vinci!"

Spaghetti, she said. *Da Vinci.* But I'm here, Mom! I am here with you, and at the same time so far away! Like everything else that's happened since the science fair experiment went haywire, that I could be seeing and hearing her here defies logic. Could Billy have made a new app without telling me, one that brings Mamma's voice to me across centuries? But how could he—he didn't even believe this jump to the past was possible.

"A voice from the future—*chi è?*"

I gasp. Leo has snuck up behind me and is looking over my shoulder. "She is calling to me?"

"Don't do that, Leo. You scared me!" I admonish him. My heart is pounding in my ears.

"Yes, Carlotta is still fixated on Leonardo da Vinci," Mamma continues. "I swear, Jules, it's like she was born into the wrong century!"

Leonardo looks puzzled as he hears his name. "How could the voice know that you—and I . . . ?"

"Yeah, well, power of imagination," I reply. I can't let on to Leonardo that this apparition, this ghost of Mamma, appears to be happening in real time . . . whatever *that* is. But if I could figure out how it works, then there's hope I could strengthen the signal and communicate with my peeps back home somehow.

Leo hesitates to marvel, then looks up at the clock that towers over Florence. "We must make haste," he says, pulling me slowly to my feet so I don't reinjure my foot. He sets off quickly toward the main piazza.

I must bring Leo and Kairos up to speed on VoIP technology enough to see what this might imply about the nature of time, or parallel universes, or . . .

Impulsively, I fish for my phone to see if there's a text or something from Billy. Nothing. But if Mom's showing up here on Zoom, or something, it must be possible to text, too.

"Did u create new video chat interface app here?" I hit send, then watch as the phone display freezes. No signal.

I slip the phone back into my backpack and again hold the tablet up to my ear.

"*Si, bueno.* Just a little tired. Jet lag, I'm sure." Mamma's still here. Or there. But I can still see her.

Weird.

"Really, Jules, I'm sure it's nothing. Yes, I promise I'll see a doctor. And please don't say anything, especially not to Carolina—the girls are probably friends on social media, and you never know what they share there. I don't want to worry Charley."

IX.
Unraveling Secrets

Not worry me! Mom's keeping a secret from me? I strain to hear more, but as we emerge into the main square, the noise around us drowns out Mamma's voice.

We never keep secrets! What if she's sick . . . ?

I wish I could just ask her what's going on. Honestly, I'm so flipped out right now. I want nothing more than to x out of this mystery app to save my battery, but I'm afraid of losing my mother.

"Mamma! What is it! You can tell me!" I yell. Several onlookers have started staring.

I hold the tablet up to my ear. I barely hear Mom ask her friend, "Can you come to the Palazzo Vecchio? Yes, the security, I know. Impossible! I will make sure they have your name. We will absolutely find time, *cara mia!*"

"More *video*, Carlotta? *Videmus?*" But of course Leo would still be eavesdropping.

"Listen, Ser Leo: I'm gonna need help to figure out a way to get back home. *Pronto. Mamma mia's* abroad with her *simfonia* and Dad's gonna have a cow!" I blurt.

Leonardo frowns. "Have . . . a cow? What is this, cow?"

"Moo!" I groan, imitating the sound. Then I point two fingers above my ears and paw at the ground. "Y'know, like *il tareau?* Anyway, it's just an expression. It means he's probably gonna be mad at me."

"I know nothing of the bullfights, but I do know my patron will also 'have a cow' when he sees a mere girl with such powerful *magico*. He will be here in due time."

"Your patron. You mean Lorenzo de' Medici?"

Might this mean that Leonardo wants to introduce little old me to the powers that be? *Il Magnifico* is reputed to have been a very forward-thinking leader in his time. It is thanks to the de' Medici family, in large part, that the Renaissance even came to be!

"He *is* the most powerful man in the *Republica*. And one of the most enlightened. You shall see. He will be most interested in your knowledge. But this tablet—we cannot give away this *misterioso* source of your knowledge without endangering you."

Apparently, this realization triggers some new calculation: Leo looks me over in the way of an artist.

"First, though, you must be dressed appropriately for an audience with *il Magnifico*. As a girl of refined temperament."

"Refined . . . um, yeah, right. I mean, have you met me?"

"*Si*. Of course I have met you." Leonardo frowns, puzzled, perhaps, at my wit. Or lack of it. They do say that humor is culturally defined, after all.

I sigh. "*Eh bene*, let's get on with it."

"Get on with what, pray tell?"

"My makeover, of course. Oh, don't get me wrong, Leo: I think it'd be cool to meet *il Magnifico*. Really! And if I could interview him, too . . ." It's hard to think anyone would doubt my story with *two* interviews with original sources.

"Also, no need to do a portrait, but if you could, you know, give me an autograph or, better yet, a cartoon to show in my report . . . but can we make it *pronto*? I'm really gonna have to eventually get back to

America before everyone starts to worry!"

It's like I can't stop spewing words, even though, the longer I talk, the more distracted Leonardo looks.

"Madonna Carlotta," Leonardo interrupts me. "I recognize your need to make haste. But I must understand more of your *sciencia* to assist you in your quest to return to America. As you came at moonlight, perhaps that is the time you must depart. And for you to reach your light speed . . . I am not certain. Tonight will be a full moon—too bright to risk shooting you in a capsule from my cannon. And I am not sure this would protect you."

"Shoot me? From your cannon? Do you mean to kill me? Seriously, Leo, I thought you were way smarter than that."

"Do you want my assistance or not, *cara?*"

"Well, yes, but I would like to live to see my own parents again."

"And believe me, I want nothing more than to honor that desire," he reassures me. "But first, you must share with me the knowledge of how you came here."

"Okay. Well, first, there's the matter of the tablet and this formula Kairos left. . . ."

"*Si*, an impressive trick! But your magic slate will not show me what has transpired in—what did you say—the *cinquecento anni* that have since passed."

"Yeah, well, that's kind of a problem of proof, isn't it? So what if I told you that in 150 years, another genius, one Sir Isaac Newton, will prove, scientifically, the law of gravity: that two objects exert a force of attraction on each other."

"Newton's *grav-i-ty*. Yes, two equal forces of nature must exert a pull, one on the other, to maintain balance. That is certain," he affirms with a wink.

It's like he really knew it all along.

I continue despite my suspicions. "What's more, when the forces of attraction are of equal mass, for every action there is an equal and opposite reaction."

By way of demonstration, I pick up a stone from the riverbed and toss it straight into the air, catch it, then arc it up in the air, watching it fall to the earth at the point it loses momentum. "Gravity. It is the proof for your calculations of trajectory from your cannon fire. You remember—last night? What goes up must come down."

"Then your coming here in time must result in an equal and opposite reaction in your own America. What is the reaction to your coming here?"

I feel my face get red. "I am gonna get in a LOT of trouble!"

Leonardo's face takes on a familiar thoughtful look. Just like in this portrait from the period—which, seeing him so close in front of me, I could swear it's a selfie.

"You must go back, then. Or what we do here will have created a ripple effect through time. That is what you are telling me, no?"

"No. Well, yes. I mean, maybe. Actually, it's a lot more complicated than that."

"Yes, I am beginning to see. And yet, it is my *filosofia* that simplicity is the ultimate sophistication."

"Don't I wish! I think this Qualia Rosetta formula—the one Kairos dropped into the cloud for me—it's got to somehow work in reverse to catapult me above the five dimensions of space-time, with a little help and a lot of luck. And then, of course, there's Lex. . . ."

I stop, seized suddenly with doubt. Because honestly, a world in which Lex Campbell kissed *me*, Charley Morton, seems a little far-fetched. "Wait a minute. Do you think this is a dream?"

Leonardo looks a little dreamy-eyed himself. "That is indeed a question I have pondered myself. Why does the eye see a thing more clearly in dreams than the imagination when awake?"

"But I am not living my dream only to wake up in a dream! Because there'd be nothing Bethy would like better than to prove I'm a dreamer who's completely unmoored from reality."

Where could Bethy really be at this moment, I wonder. That's when I hear a ping. If I didn't know better, I'd think someone was texting me. But I dare not look at my phone.

"Elisabetta? She is your friend?"

"Why do I feel like I'm on *Candid Camera*? Okay. Time's up."

"Time *is* up, Signorina, though I'm afraid there is no *camera obscura* here, except the one that brought you to me to change our conception of the physical world forever. And, I am sorry to say, I don't know the way back. Even if we had such tools as might carry you forward using the Qualia Rosetta formula you suggest, we would need to harness extraordinary sources of power to activate any real *machina ex tempora* like the one that brought you here."

"But I built the machine from your plans! If it worked once, surely we can re-create the equivalent based on modern science, and your own invention. . . ."

"Is it not still true in your time that nature is the source of all true knowledge? She has her own logic, her own laws; she has no effect without cause nor invention without necessity."

Something he's saying: laws of nature. Necessity as the mother of invention. Mother! At the renewed thought of her possibly being ill, or maybe even dying, I let go, unable to control myself.

"*Si*, Ser Leonardo. This is necessity! It is *absolutamente necessario* for me to figure out a way to get back in time!"

I feel my eyes beginning to drip at the corners and pass a sleeve hastily over my face. I can't lose it here. Not in front of my Renaissance idol.

"Tears come from the heart and not the brain, Signorina," he cautions me, handing me what appears to a be semi-clean cloth to blow my nose.

"Sit, Carlotta. Crying does not advance one's ability to see for the first time what has never before been seen."

I force myself to take a few deep breaths. Mamma has been trying to get me to practice mindfulness for*ever*. After a long moment, I feel as though I might be able to think a little clearer.

"Thanks, Ser Leonardo," I say, gratefully handing him back the cloth. "*Mi sento più sereno*. If we might put our heads together—maybe let's bring Kairos into it—he's a brainiac. I must figure out a way to reverse the arrow of time!"

"Now, Signorina *mia*," Leonardo says, in a more comforting tone, "I will need time to design such a machine with power to—as your Newton might say—bend the arc of time. It is but the seed of an idea and, like a seed, must be nurtured to grow. With time and attention, it may flower."

"What? You're joking." But he appears not to be joking. "Am I stuck here until then?"

"Like a moth in amber. At least for now. I feel there must be more of your knowledge that I need to acquire. You will teach me."

"But you are the teacher, Maestro! I'm just a humble student."

"Poor is the pupil who does not surpass her master. I will let my mind rest on this puzzle, and this I cannot do without time. But we must find a suitable costume and a story for your presence before others question your being here."

Time, time, time: All is changed with time. Yet it would seem time is not on my side.

X.

Technology Changes Everything

"**H**ome." I'm not even sure Maryland—in the land of the free and the home of the brave—is the ultimate destination now. "What with Mamma in Florence . . ."

"Can you show me your home?" Leonardo asks. His accent cracks me up.

I just don't know anymore, whether the simplest of requests could distort the whole of history from this time forward. I rummage through my backpack, dumping out the detritus (a fancy word for junk) of another century: Da Vinci Middle School fleece, paper clips, granola bar, Goldfish cracker crumbs, pencil stubs, the real earbuds—for listening to music. Juice boxes! I'm so thirsty, I smack my lips at something so mundane as apple juice, and quick as my fumbling fingers allow, I stick a straw in the juice packet and start sucking. And then I remember my manners and hold one out to Leonardo, who's looking at me like the crazy person I suppose I am here.

"*Questo?*" he asks.

"A drink. Try it!" He starts to imitate me, sucking hard on the straw. After a minute or two, I notice the look on his face is the same one I associate with a kid who's eaten through all his Halloween candy in one sitting.

"It's okay," I try to assure him. "I know there's a lot of sugar in it but you'll get used to it. Believe me."

He clearly has no idea what I'm talking about, but I can see the sugar high hit its mark. All of a sudden, Leonardo is grabbing for my tablet.

"Hey, don't break it," I yell, grabbing it back. "That's my lifeline!"

But Leonardo is acting like a man possessed. I can see the only way out is through—I'll have to show him where home is. Photos, anyway.

I sigh, wondering again at the possibility of creating a paradox to a future where I no longer live as me.

"Here are some of my pictures of home. Takoma Park, Maryland. United States of America. *Il Nuovo Mundi*." I pull up my photos of home. There's the house, and the swings in the backyard. I take a breath, realizing how far away all that is, and begin to swipe through quickly.

"That's my mom." I have to stop when I see her. I snapped that shot while we were supposed to be practicing violin together. She's deep in concentration: that was before she got mad at me for not coming in right away at my part—too busy taking her picture. I touch the screen pretending I can feel her face, and despite trying to be brave, my eyes are welling up again.

But Leonardo is too fascinated by the technology to notice.

"*Dio!* The camera—what realism this could allow us for painting!" He examines one photo after another: my parents, Billy, Beth. Our new Prius in the driveway.

"It's a car," I begin. "*Automobile?* One drives it, like a horseless carriage." I pinch the image to enlarge it on the screen.

"*Auto-mo-bile. Si.* I would design something like this!" he exclaims. Then he starts swiping faster, his eyes wide, as if seeing new possibilities.

"I have tried with my writings to capture the fundamental connections between all things—painting, *sculptura, scientia, invention* . . . *canali . . . carta* . . . but your *camera?* This is not art!"

"Yeah, um . . . no. Well, it's art of sorts. Photography, we call it. *La fotografia?*"

He shakes his head, disapproving. "The artist must see and interpret to the canvas what he sees! To have a machine that reproduces the scene . . . this is the work of a scribe, not an artist."

Although this academic discussion might be interesting in another place and time, I don't really feel as if debating Leonardo da Vinci on the nature of art would be in my best interest.

"There are other things my machine, as you call it, can show us!" I pull up the Renaissance Google Earth project I worked on for social studies. I was so proud of the A I got on this project; I put a ton of effort into it.

"So, if you notice, we can search for points of interest and historical facts to see the advances during your time. We can even check out where we are right now, Leonardo, at the Palazzo Vecchio. If we could look a few months ahead," which I note to my own regret that we cannot, "news flash: Your *Magnifico* dies at the mercy of his nemesis . . . the Pope is . . ."

"*Nuovo mundi?* And, you dare tell me, Lorenzo de' Medici dies! I am not aware of any illness. And he is to die, you say, in his enemy's arms?

"NO! I cannot see this . . . this blasphemy!"

I disregard his tone. "Oh, yeah, and wait—I have to show you this. We discovered it not too long ago in my time: a map of the world you or some artisan in your workshop apparently etch—wait for it—on an ostrich egg. A kind of 'Eggle' Earth."

"*Ma, che sei grullo!*" He stares at the etching, like this is the stupidest idea for a map he's ever seen. "The world . . . in an egg?"

"No, seriously, Leo. I kid you not! Well, of course, you don't know it yet, but Columbus does indeed prove that the Earth is round: thus, the egg. And in the place of Asia, you guys write, 'Here Are Dragons!'"

"*Hic Sunt Dracones? A Terra Incognito!* And be there, in fact, dragons . . . ?"

The Maestro appears at a loss for words. This previewing the future is kinda fun—and scary. I take a half skip to get us physically moving again.

But Leonardo seems to tap into my concern about how seeing into the future might change it. "What has not happened cannot be prede-termined. I will not allow it."

What can I say? "Not sure anyone can stop the future, Leo. But I will not show you any more if you do not wish to see it, except to bring up the obvious point that, if I stay, who knows what weirdness might happen."

He nods. And then, as if he can't help himself, "Just one more thing I would like to know. What of the *scultore* . . . what of Michelangelo Buonarroti?"

"Oh, also a genius! He gets commissioned by Rome to paint—but wait, I can show you his incredible masterpiece." I scroll to find an e-book on European history and find a photo of the Sistine Chapel.

"*Buonarroti. Il Papa. A Roma,*" Leonardo mutters. "He will despise this commission!" His fingers trace arcs across the screen, following the lines of the great windows of the Sistine. But as I watch his long, grace-ful fingers, I freeze in my tracks. The lines in the illustration begin to vanish as he touches them!

"Holy Michelangelo!" I gasp. "It's all disappearing! One of the most famous works of art in the world!" I try quickly closing the e-book and reopening it.

Michelangelo's outline is gone. Just like that, the world famous biblical creation scene on the dome of the Sistine Chapel is erased.

"I need to sit," I say, suddenly dizzy. Leonardo must be worried about me now, because he leads me to sit on the edge of a fountain in a large open square.

We must have reached the center of town. Statesmen-like men and elegant women are milling around us, but I can hardly focus. Breathing hard, I have to put my head down on my arms until, after a few minutes, I feel composed enough to sit up and look around.

"Where on earth are we?"

"Ecco Palazzo della Signoria," Leonardo informs me, and I have to put my head down again. "And your time," he points to the clock, with its single hand. *"Ecco."*

"You mean the Palazzo Vecchio?" I ask. If it's true, this "Old Palace" is where Mamma has plans to meet her friend Giuliana later. Much later. I look around for visual clues: It could fit with the photos I've seen, except with a lot fewer sculptures. I suppose many wouldn't have been created yet.

"This is the seat of government, the seat *della Republica di Firenze*, Carlotta. And the many outstanding guilds are housed here, including my own, The Guild of Saint Luke, for artisans of all skills—stonework, sculpting, painting, murals. As for your query, I know of no 'old palace' here in Firenze."

"Yeah, well, it may not be 'old' to you, but it's ancient history to me!" I retort, frustrated at the whole parallel time theme that seems to be playing out here.

"Signorina?" says Leonardo solicitously. "Why be angry? Is it your ankle that bothers you?" He touches my foot gently, and I shake my head. My foot does hurt. My head, too. I am so tired. And hungry. And lost.

Leonardo unwraps the linen from my foot. There are bruises all around my ankle, and it still looks swollen. Probably from walking.

"Where is young Kairos?!" Leonardo looks around the square, as if expecting his apprentice to have ESP. "He will have your salve in his possession. The boy has a habit of disappearing at just such moments as he is needed!"

Hearing this diatribe, I realize it was Kairos who led me here. Kairos who understands who I am and where I come from. Kairos who is my only hope to get out of this. And now he, too, is missing in action!

Leonardo softens, patting me awkwardly on the head. "O, *cara mia*. Fear not. All will be well! You are safe."

I attempt to put on my brave face.

It's then I notice the sights and sounds all around me. A cock crows in the distance. A woman scats a noisy dog from her courtyard and some-one close by throws dirty water out a second-story window, drenching two boys playing tag.

The square is alive with color, with light, with sound. The costumes are amazing. Except they're really everyday dress. Not only the women—men, too, are decked out in finery, jewels, wigs, and furs.

My scan is arrested by two mountain-high pyramids of stuff glittering in the corners of the square. The scene reminds me of something, but I can't pull the connection out of my memory.

Still, the square offers a real feast for the eyes! I can see where Botticelli, Michelangelo, Raphael, Caravaggio, and Leonardo himself find their inspiration.

And music! Singers, flutes, drums, a madrigal. Such a cacophony! (That means loud, dissonant sounds, sort of like a cringeworthy middle school marching band—I know you know what I mean!) I am not even sure all those instruments are playing in tune with each other, much less the voices. Leonardo, I note, is tapping his feet in time to the music.

"I will return anon." Leonardo hands me my tablet—I forgot he still had it. He strides across the square, seeming quick to abandon me.

"Wait, where are you going, Leo?" But he's already out of earshot.

I caress my treasure, the tablet that ties me to the family I was born to, wondering if Spotify would play some melody to remind me. Since Leonardo has dashed off, I quick extract my normal earbuds from the pocket of my backpack and swap them out for Translator. Careful to pull my hair down so no one notices, I turn up the volume again, in case . . . in case. . . .

And then, I hear my mother's voice again. I look down at the tablet, hoping beyond hope to see my *cara mamma*'s face. Wondering at how she might be so near, and yet so far.

"Giuliana? *Si, bueno.* If nothing else, let's shoot for a cappuccino."

Uno miracolo. I can see her walking. Mom pans to the scene around her, I guess to show Giuliana where she is standing, and there is the same clock tower behind her, chiming the hour. And a fountain. This very fountain!

As I see we are in the same place, I wonder: Could a syncing of hour, day, and place trigger a synchronous (hard to wrap your head around this word, which refers to events existing or occurring at the same time) expression of energy across time? Weirder things have been known to happen!

Here and now, I catch a glimpse of myself reflected in the fountain—wild hair, weird dress, anxious eyes rippling amid the splashing waters—and I wish Mamma could peer into *her* fountain there and see my image here. And I swear, for a nanosecond I can see her reflection in this pool in front of me, putting her arm around my shoulders and touching her belly. And for an instant, under the warm spell of that illusion, I have hope.

Then, in a splash, it is gone. Mamma's face disappears from the screen. Instead, I catch a glimpse of the statue on top of the fountain in Mamma's view, so different than the one above my head. In Mom's view, there's a statue of a giant naked man with a beard!

"Oh, gross!"

"Gross?" I hadn't noticed all the people milling around within earshot. A girl with big black eyes, wearing a blue-gray woolen dress and a white cotton cap over her dark hair—she looks to be about eight—has been watching me in the square. There's something familiar about her face; in my current state of mind, I can't put my finger on it.

"Gross?" she exclaims, louder this time, rolling her *r*'s the way the Italians do.

"Shh!" I put my finger up to my mouth, and she hisses back the same way. She's mocking me!

"What is your name?" I ask. *"Tua nomme?"*

"Carolina!" she replies, louder now. Then she points at me and says, slyly, "Carlotta! *Pomodoro? Es rosso!*" She giggles.

That's where I recognize her—from Signora Vincenzo's *taverna*!

"Oh, about that whole tomato thing. Yeah, well . . . anyway, just call me Charley."

"Tcharrrr-li," she repeats, with that same rolling *r*. *"Tcharrr-li, te amo."*

She loves me, she says. I suddenly glom on to this like a lifeline. Some regular person here cares about me—when she's not mocking me, that is. I could use a real friend here. I mean, Kairos may be closer to my age, but I'm not quite sure I can trust him. The more I think about it, the more I suspect he's hiding something from me.

But there's nothing hidden about Carolina. She skips around the fountain, dipping her fingers in to splash me; I wish I could splash and play, too. But I have to act my age, or Leonardo won't take me seriously.

I slap her hand in a high-five as she skips by. "Hey, cutie—do you think . . . I mean, maybe you could show me . . . that is, help me find what I'm looking for?"

At first Carolina looks puzzled, until I realize she probably doesn't understand a word I'm saying. I quick take out my earbuds and put Translator back on.

"Tcharrr-li, *Voi mi insegnerà?*" And here, she mimes the stern lecture of a teacher.

"Will I teach you?!" I interpret. "Surely, you have your own teachers, Carolina."

"No," she replies. "I am a servant in the household of Vincenzo!"

A servant! At a tavern! How can that be? She's way too young to be hanging out in bars.

Before I can ask the question, she pulls my hand, the one that has been cradling the tablet under my cloak. "*Tua strega, no?!* Show me your magic glass!"

She thinks I'm a witch!

"Shh! You must keep quiet about this, Carolina!" I hiss, nervous at the crowds. There are ears here!

"Shh!" she hisses back, with a mischievous grin. I wave my free hand at her, which sends a flock of pigeons fluttering in my face. When the bird cloud clears, she is gone.

"Carolina? Where . . . ?" I pause to listen; no response. "Phew!" I say under my breath, as Leonardo comes near again. "Close call!"

Leonardo carries his lute. "*Tutti bene,* Carlotta?" he asks with some concern.

If he only knew.

I need to stay as under-the-radar as possible—not an easy feat, given that Leonardo is something of a celebrity, even now, with his beautiful face and easy charm. He might even be considered "The Beeb" of his day, although Justin's talents don't approach those of the Maestro. And what does that say for the state of modern civilization?!

Strumming the lute, Leonardo has attracted something of a crowd. Some roaming musicians begin to gather around him. Madrigal singers appear to be improvising their harmonies. At least that's how the odd intervals sound to me. The square is practically vibrating, with bystanders stopping to listen before continuing on their way.

This is a fortunate turn of events for my purposes. I can turn up the volume on my tablet a bit, masked as it is by lute, piccolo, and voices, and I dare to lower my eyes to watch what's unfolding in that future piazza, my mother's present, in real time.

As I watch what is being captured and somehow transmitted by my mom's phone, I can see the arriving NSO musicians in jeans and T-shirts filing into the palace behind my mom, carrying their instruments, and Mamma, walking inside with them. Inside the Palazzo Vecchio, the scene is alive with stagehands in hardhats and musicians finalizing the setup for their concert. I hear various instruments being tuned up in the background.

"We will find time, *cara mia!*" Mom assures Giuliana before the screen goes dark.

But I am her *cara mia*! I am here! Can you hear me? Mamma, why can't I talk to you?!

XI.
The Art of Diplomacy

I don't get any time to ponder this predicament: Some official-looking person is approaching on horseback, undoubtedly attracted by the commotion. I quickly stuff my "magic slate" into my backpack and throw the cape over it for protection.

While the musicians and townspeople continue their version of a flash mob, Leonardo inches close enough to whisper in my ear. "Carlotta, *il Magnifico* approaches." He looks me up and down and tsk-tsks me. "That dress! Alas, I should have proffered a more suitable costume from my atelier. I keep them for the models who sit for me. *Un vero peccato.*" He sighs and nudges me to watch as he performs a little two-step in time to the music. "A courtier to sovereigns must present herself properly."

"Courtier?! But I'm not courting anybody!" I announce loudly, over the din.

"Lorenzo de' Medici demands our respect," he repeats without missing a step. I watch as the citizens of Florence, now clearing a parade path, begin to do what looks like the wave, bowing to *il Magnifico*.

"Why's everybody doing that now?" I ask. "Is that part of your act?"

"There are formalities you must follow if you are to be introduced in the court of Lorenzo de' Medici, *cara* Carlotta," he says, handing off his lute to another musician in the passing parade. "The proper bow or curtsy is essential. Follow my lead." Again, he dances, while reciting, "Left foot forward, left foot back. Bend both knees. Then straighten and bring both feet together."

So that's what everyone is doing? I may have been blessed with many talents, but dancing is not one of them. I try to follow his feet, but my ankle still aches, and this darned skirt is so long! I try to keep up without toppling, but my feet get caught in the hem. Leonardo grabs my elbow, just in time to avoid a face-plant. Some first impression!

"Oops, sorry, Ser Leonardo!" I have to show a little respect, what with the crowd around, even though Leo and I are now on a first-name basis. "I'm such a klutz!"

Wonder if Leo knows about the 10,000 hours rule. He has clearly practiced a lot. Although, the way things look now, I may, in fact, have centuries to rehearse the courtier's bow!

Apparently, the foot shuffle curtsy's only part of the proper show of courtesy. (Funny, these words sound suspiciously close to "courtesan." I make a mental note to check out the connection.) Distracted, I don't notice the hush that's fallen over the crowd until my third attempt at

the bow, which doesn't go much better than the first two. Leonardo changes places to jump in front of me, breaking my concentration.

"After me, Carlotta," Leonardo commands, now adding in a hand motion. I try to imitate this new step, but the hand gesture completely throws off my footing, landing me on my tush.

"Ugh!" I gulp, after which I hear the crowd gasp.

"Who's the girl who stumbles before me?" A deep, commanding voice pierces the air, but I can't quite tell from where.

"*Magnifico!*" exclaims Leonardo, as he bows even deeper, this time from the waist and with a flourish of the hand.

I'm sure my face must be turning three shades of red. I scramble unceremoniously to my feet and sneak a glance upward. Lorenzo's up on his high horse. Literally! And no Macaroni, this one, but a great white steed with a red and gold harness and regal trappings, a coterie of henchmen trailing ceremonially behind him just like you'd see in a movie.

"Allow me to present Carlotta, a fair maiden and visitor from afar to our fair Firenze, *Magnifico.*"

This time, I manage to stay on my feet while bowing.

The big man barely glances at me. "Pray tell, whence do you harken, Madonna?"

"Um . . . er . . ." I've forgotten my alibi.

"She hails from the north, *Magnifico*," Leonardo chimes in, saving me.

"I am here to see the wonders of your city, *Magnifico*, and learn as much as I can from the Maestro," I reply in the closest version to the truth I can conjure out of my confusion.

"Ah," he nods. "While our city is a model of learning, that is for the men. A gentle maiden would not act so brazenly in the public square."

I find condescension hard to swallow. "Brazen? I have every right—!" I start to exclaim, but Leonardo squeezes my arm.

"No matter." Lorenzo waves me off. "I have business with the *artista*. Da Vinci, what delays your delivering the 'magic' missiles you promised me a fortnight past?"

"Alas, *Magnifico*, disappointing news on that front, as even the gentle maiden here will attest. I fear her welcome here last night was marred by a misfiring of my cannon."

"Oh, no. Not again, da Vinci! Another misfire?" Lorenzo roars, dismounting, and waving his horsemen away. "No more excuses! I advance you enough gold florins to finance ten armies, and yet, you still cannot manage to finish even one commission in the defense of this Republic!"

I feel bad for Leonardo. He's been so nice to me. He really was trying with the whole night warfare thing, and it was probably my fault that he couldn't test out his new weapons properly. To distract Lorenzo from his anger, I jump in, as only seems polite.

"Honored, Signor de' Medici! *In veritatis!*"

In truth. How dumb does that sound?! If Translator is supplying the right words, my ears are having a hard time discerning them, what with all the commotion and my heart beating in my ears. A smattering of first-year Latin from last week's vocabulary test is all I can come up with right now.

To cover up, I attempt the courtier's bow again, stumbling a little less this time.

Leonardo shoots me a wink and I manage to give him a secret smile in return.

"How now? The *ragazza* refuses to stay silent!" Lorenzo pinches me hard on the tush.

"Hey, buddy, cool it! You have no right to put your hands on me!" I shriek. *Magnifico* or no, I really wanna sock him one.

In a flash, Leonardo pulls me aside. "Stay your tongue, girl. In this place, the ruler has every right," he whispers, "or you'll find your fate that of scullery maid by day and Lorenzo's muse by night."

Clearly more info than I signed up for, but now that Leo's laid out the consequences, I get this game. I execute my curtsy again—the only way I can think to wriggle civilly out of *il Magnifico*'s grip.

But the damage is done. Lorenzo draws up to his full height and peers down at me, considering, as if I am but a pawn to be moved around his chessboard at will.

"What say you, wench? What words are these that have power to stay my hands from my property?"

This is too much. "Property! Say, who the hell do you think you are, anyway?!"

There are "oohs" and "aahs" from the crowd around us now, and calls for a fight; Leonardo, as a gentleman, would apparently be expected to defend my honor, even before a nobleman such as Lorenzo.

But instead, Leonardo places a gentle hand on my arm even as he bows once more. "*Il Magnifico*, you have been most generous to the loyal citizens of Firenze and particularly this humble servant. Forgive this girl. Fair Carlotta deserves forgiveness for her ignorance. She hails from that tribe of barbarians to the North!"

Lorenzo apparently feels this is no excuse. "Even the Germanic tribes honor the graces of nobility!"

In the distance I spy Kairos striding purposefully toward us, a serious look on his face. Skipping in quick step behind him to keep up is none other than Carolina.

"Do you have knowledge of this girl?" Kairos calls out, drawing the attention of the crowd and looking at me accusatorily. Carolina hides behind his pantaloons, then peeks out at me slyly. "My sister tells me you have been teaching her of your foreign ways. She demands to—*como se dice*—'play' with you, Carlotta. What have you to say about this!"

I am astonished that playing might be considered a punishable offense, and that Kairos, of all people, would accuse me! I start to object until Leo pinches me on the arm and nods toward Lorenzo who, attention wandering, clearly has no interest in child's play.

"*Si*, we were playing. But I didn't know she was your sister, Kairos." Although, now that I think about it, I notice a resemblance. "*Ciao, bella* Carolina."

"*He-ii, Tcharr-li*," she enunciates, giggling.

"Carolina!" Kairos, looking serious, puts two fingers to her nose and tweaks it. "What has *nostra madre* told you about shirking your responsibilities to the family?!"

But it doesn't matter, 'cause Carolina and I, we share a secret. I wink, and Carolina tries winking back, putting her finger over one eye, then the other.

"Do not waste my time with such nonsense!" Lorenzo grunts. He then begins to pontificate to the crowd, as befits a Medici.

I lean in close enough to Kairos that we cannot be heard as Lorenzo continues to impress upon the crowd his beneficence as their ruler.

"Hey, where've you been, dude? You might've given me a heads-up of the dangers here for a foreigner and a girl."

Speechifying over, I see Lorenzo turn and begin to parade back toward the Palazzo Vecchio, the crowd closing in behind him.

"Dangers?" Kairos says, saluting at Lorenzo's fading back. "What danger could come to a *filia dei* Renaissance?"

"Me, a daughter of the Renaissance . . . if my mom ever heard you say that, she'd—"

"Have a *cow*?" Leonardo injects with a sly smile, ever so reminiscent of the Mona Lisa.

"I am no cow!" I quip. "Nor a girl of the fifteenth century. You've got it all wrong, Kairos."

"Does he?" Leonardo says. "If I were to judge, you would do well to take his observations to heart. For it is true, is it not: One can have no smaller or greater mastery than mastery of oneself."

I get it: A girl who keeps a low profile won't outshine *il Magnifico*, in all his splendor. Even if I have to fake it.

Carolina tags me, as if starting a game of duck-duck-goose, then begins singing in a light, lilting voice:

> *Coloro che cercano, trovare la gioia oggi,*
> *domani non comporta alcune verità.*
> Let those who seek, find joy today,
> tomorrow brings no certain truth.
> Everyone play music, dance, and sing!
> The heart burns with sweetness!
> No toil and no pain!
> That what must be, it had better be.
> Let those who seek, find joy today,
> tomorrow brings no certain truth.

"Carolina, that's a beautiful song," I exclaim.

"*Si, una bella canzone. Grazie, Carlotta.*" The little girl hides her giggle. "*È la canzone dei Magnifico.*" She tags me again.

"Lorenzo's song?" I ask. "He composes music?" This is not a fact we learned in social studies. "I also have composed a *canzone* myself with *mia mamma*—'Leo,' it is called." At this, I feel myself blushing. Because that was before I went on this celebrity hunt, and I don't want Leonardo to think I'm a fangirl, or anything.

"If I only had my violin here, I could play you all a few bars."

Kairos whispers again in my ear. "*Scusi,* Carlotta. Be aware that here, your violin has yet to be invented!"

"Huh? No violin?" Not sure why, but I take this news personally.

"*Si,* you must play for us, Carlotta!" Carolina insists, smiling and waving my tablet openly.

The little scamp! In tagging me, she apparently pinched the tablet out of my backpack! Now aware of the danger of Lorenzo's spies, I look around to make sure there's no one besides us who is watching.

"Carolina, no! Give it back!" I cry.

But she is already shaking and twisting it, tapping and swiping at the screen before I can wrestle it away. She must've found my music, and immediately, my "Leo" recording starts up. "Too loud!"

The commotion has attracted Lorenzo's attention back in our direction. He pulls his horse around, confounding his retinue.

"What instrument does the girl play here, pray tell?" he asks.

Carolina ignores him, staring intently at the screen.

"Give it back, Carolina!" I shout in a panic. If this technology and the knowledge it contains were to fall into the hands of one so powerful as the de' Medici family, all of history could be erased in one fell swipe.

But it is too late. Lorenzo motions to one of his men to grab the screen from Carolina's hand. Lorenzo digs his heels into his restive horse—high above the curious eyes of his courtiers—peers at the screen, then glances from me to Leonardo, and back at the screen.

It's then I hear a boom, reminiscent of Leonardo's cannon firing, coming from my tablet. What is he seeing? I jump up and down, trying to get a peek at the screen.

"Where did you get this?" Lorenzo demands of Carolina. She shrugs.

"It is simply a tablet, Ser Lorenzo," ventures Kairos. "It is a *modello* by Ser Leonardo—one of many rude prototypes to display *Magnifico's* generous commissions."

Slowly gaining comprehension, Lorenzo gives my tablet to Leonardo, who immediately registers Carolina's brilliant trick.

"I told you I have been working on this, *Magnifico!*"

"Is this the armament you have been experimenting with on our behalf, da Vinci?"

Leonardo hands me back the tablet. Glancing quickly, I see a sketch for the tri-barrel cannon he was firing this morning (was it just this morning?) when I, unexpectedly, dropped in.

I immediately shove my device back in my backpack and rearrange the cape to hide it. "How did you—?" I ask, with a scolding glance at Carolina. But she keeps her eyes cast down, seemingly fascinated by her foot as it traces the cobblestones in the piazza.

"*Precisemente, Magnifico!*" Leo grins. "A multibarreled munition to add to your cavalry. As I mentioned, I was testing its accuracy the night Carlotta came to us."

"It looks like a machine gun," I murmur, then catch myself.

"Why did you not say so earlier, da Vinci?" says Lorenzo, apparently well satisfied. "Then our investment is not completely in vain! I must see this new weapon for myself."

"Of course, Maestro," says Leonardo, with a glance in my direction. "When it is ready to demonstrate. I have only a *modello*, here. A moving

cartoon is not yet a 'machine gun,' as our visitor has named it."

Apparently, this reminds Lorenzo that he has unfinished business with me.

"I warn you, *ragazza*." Lorenzo wags his finger in front of my face. "In this place, modesty is a virtue. Remember, a stranger in Firenze is welcome as long as she respects our ways."

"Modest—what?" I look down to confirm: I'm covered pretty much head to toe.

"And you, da Vinci, if I catch you delaying my project further, it will be your none-too-humble head mounted over the piazza for all to jeer at."

Chastened, I try a more modest tone. "*Si, milord.* You must forgive me, for I was startled by your magnificence. I will be about my business now."

Leonardo seems relieved. "*Bene.* Kairos, you will go back to my studio to find the drawings for this *machine gun*, as Carlotta calls it. I must have a private word with *Magnifico.*"

"Andiamos, Carolina." Kairos moves quickly to collar Carolina, who whimpers as he pushes her ahead of him.

Leonardo again whispers, "Hide yourself, Madonna. You must not reveal yourself to *Magnifico* again. Meet me beneath the Ponte Vecchio at noontide. Hide in the shadows beneath the bridge and wait for the strains of my lute before you venture into daylight. In privacy, we may set our minds to your return to America."

Kairos hesitates. "If you keep your wits about you, Carlotta, you will be safe. Simply follow the Maestro's instructions."

I look from Kairos to Leonardo: I'm a little anxious about my ability to stick to Leonardo's plan, what with all the twists and turns through alleys and snaking streets it's taken us to get this far.

But on one point, I am satisfied: confirmation that Leo will let me in on his secrets. I mean, it's taken me centuries to get this far—I'm not going home without the treasure that brought me here in the first place.

"Prego, Ser Leonardo, before I go, would you oblige me with an interview? I must learn your secret: How you are able to master, well, everything, and so far ahead of your time? The science! Maps, art, architecture, canals!"

Leo looks up, as above the *Campanile,* a falcon circles lazily. Does he find answers written in the sky?

"Beware what you wish for, Carlotta. Truth comes at a cost far darker than faded dreams on waking."

What's that supposed to mean, I wonder? *Misterioso.*

"Ser Leonardo!" Lorenzo is evidently not accustomed to being kept waiting. His courtiers magically reassemble around him. "By Jupiter, we have business we must attend to."

Again, the crowd makes way. Everyone but Leonardo falls in line behind Lorenzo. Spying me out of the corner of his eye, he bellows, "And you would do well to make haste that this young mistress, she with the moving screen, vanish quickly . . . or she will need to answer to me!"

Lorenzo's men, hands on swords and knives gleaming silvery in their hilts, follow the Magnificent One, their steely, suspicious stares creeping me out as they file past me in the piazza.

Leonardo looks to me expectantly. "Have you not heard *Magnifico's* warning? You must vanish, presto, Carlotta."

Presto, change-o. Would that it were that easy, but my feet seem to have taken root in the piazza.

"I've forgotten where to begin. Can't you take me to where I need to be? *Prego*, Ser Leonardo?" I hear myself beg. I think the shock of all that's happened is beginning to set in.

But Leonardo has already begun filing in behind Lorenzo's parade. Turning, he points toward the Arno, and offers me yet another riddle. "Your magic box of tricks contains both past and future. Though the way home is not yet in evidence, we will uncover instructions to send you forward in time."

The anxiety of not knowing where I am—or where I am to go—is getting the best of me. Being part of the parade, where I can blend in with the crowd and follow Leonardo, feels safer than being alone trying to find my way around the circuitous alleyways of Florence in the bright light of day. I tag along behind Leonardo, following with the crowd as best as possible. I aim to try to keep the conversation with Leonardo flowing to avoid drawing further attention.

"Why do you remain, Carlotta?" Leo says, finally, after I tug on his voluminous sleeve one too many times so as not to get swallowed in the *défilé* (a French word for parade; but more of that for another day). "Did you not hear? You are in danger!"

"Yeah, gotcha. But my magic box, as you call it. I just wanted to show you . . ." Having gotten his attention again, I unzip my backpack and peek again at my tablet. The screen is now black. Has it gone dead?

"It's a black box for now," I inform him. "I'll need time to set up my solar battery to recharge. Unless you have a spare Pentium processor?"

Leonardo looks puzzled. "I fear that my lack of understanding has more to do with modernity than linguistic deficiency. What is a Pentium, pray tell? *Armatura* of five sides, no doubt?"

I laugh. "Oh, we have that, too. The Pentagon. It's a huge, ginormous building to house the Department of Defense. In America."

"It stores all America's weapons, then? This I would see."

"No, no—the Pentium is something embedded in a computer that improves processing speed—oh, never mind. It's too complicated to explain!"

"What a complex world you must live in, Carlotta! So, your *sol-ar bat-ter-y:* This must power a weapon?"

"And other things. I mean, without coal or gas-generated electricity, I have to make do." I fish Billy's solar battery from my backpack. "See? This tool is designed to capture the sun's energy. A battery stores power and the panel that is attached—it magnifies the sun's rays. Old Sol should be strong enough soon. By midday, with enough luck . . ."

"Time stays long enough for those who use it," observes Leonardo.

At that moment Carolina runs up. Kairos, taking giant steps, is close on her heels.

The little girl grips my hand. "Do not worry, you are not alone here, Carlotta! We are friends now!"

"*Grazie*, Carolina! I am happy to have you as a friend."

"*Ecco, Carolina.* You scamp!" Kairos glances at me, acknowledging he's used this new word correctly, and grabs Carolina's other hand. Immediately, the girl starts hopping up and down, giving us her weight as she kicks both feet into the air.

For one brief moment, this feels like family. Carolina skips, pulling us forward, and tries to get Leonardo to join us in our game. "*Evviva!* We fly!" she shouts.

Leonardo shakes her off abruptly. "I regret, *cara* Carolina. I will fly with you another time. *Il Magnifico* beckons. Carlotta, I will fetch you ere midday. Remember—await my signal beneath the Ponte Vecchio."

"*Andiamo,* Carolina." Kairos tugs his sister by the hand. "We must be off and leave Carlotta. She has embarked on a long journey; her path lies in the detours."

More cryptic remarks. I look from Leonardo to Kairos for an explanation.

"Kairos, hold up. Before you go—I want to give you this." I offer him the tablet and my makeshift solar panel. "Can you set it up in the best position to capture the sun? It needs to be recharged if I ever hope to reconnect with my world."

Kairos takes it from my hand. "*Si,* Carlotta. *No problema.* Remember, you hold the key—it, too, shines golden as the sun. And its power is nearly as potent."

His words barely register in my exploding brain. All I know is, this is one strange land, and these people are stranger still.

"But the tablet—Kairos, you are not to let it out of your sight! PLEASE! It is more valuable to me than all the florins in Florence. As soon as it holds enough charge, I want you to bring it back to me." I hesitate, realizing I don't know where I'm going to be. And no cell reception. No phones at all!

"Wait . . . how will you find me?"

Carolina gives my left hand a squeeze and smiles up at me. "Fear not, we will find you, *amica!* And do not worry about your mamma, or anything that might befall you here. We are friends forever! I will not let Kairos fail in this mission. We will see each other again soon! *Te amo, Tcharr-li.*"

I love you. These words are a balm to my soul. I squeeze back. "High five!" I clap my right hand with hers, and smile at that impish face. What she doesn't know! What none of us do! I am more than a little afraid.

I realize that in her eager greeting, Carolina has squeezed something in my hand that is still curled inside my fist. I unclench my fist to see: the golden compass is shining, *como del sol.*

"Our detours are our journeys," I echo, as Carolina and Kairos walk away. "Oh, God, I hope I can figure it out!"

Still standing beside me, Leonardo touches a finger to his head, and then to mine. "We will learn together, Carlotta. Now, go! Before Lorenzo returns and sees how you tarry!"

XII.
The Slip of a Ribbon

I'm so thirsty! What I wouldn't give for a bottle of filtered H_2O, with or without the fluoride. I catch a glimmer of the sun-speckled river in the distance as I trace a serpentine path to the Arno, darting from street to alleyway.

This mid-morning sun is hot, even in March. I pull the hood off; I don't even care if it kills my cover. I wonder if I'm headed toward the right "old" bridge, where Leo has promised to meet up with me.

Honestly, though, I can see what Carolina meant about finding me wherever I might be: Firenze feels like a small town, and I can almost feel the whispers of nosy neighbors, the eyes of spies creeping behind me through the alleyways.

Walking through the ancient city, I can't help but think about the last time I visited my own city, Washington, D.C., with Dad and Billy. It was hot that day last fall (was it just last fall?!), when we saw the Leonardo exhibit, the moment that set this impossible quest in motion. On the wide-open spaces of the Mall, there were kids playing, couples kissing, busy people in business suits looking all official. The scenery I'm passing through here is not much different, except the fashions are kind of atrocious, if I do say, with men in gaudy pantaloons and women wearing fine linens and a cover of silks in a rainbow of colors. For the peasants, the look is what I can only describe as vintage burlap sack.

The contrast between wealth and poverty looks pretty extreme—lace, gold, and grand palaces versus plain, coarse-woven cloth and drafty fleapits where the common people must live. I guess that's what the grownups in my day are talking about when they fuss and worry about the "growing inequality of wealth."

To my eye, the real disparity is between the picture-postcard perfection of official Florence and the dirty town I experience. Outside the main piazzas and central areas around the *Signoria* is this—a gray zone, I'll call it—overhung with laundry drying, people spilling out pails of who knows what into the street from second-story windows, and soot-covered walls. I find myself stepping over manure, feral cats, and other things I can't identify.

It does make me curious about the spread of disease, what with no handwashing, sewage in the streets, and people bathing—when they *do* bathe—in a horse trough.

It's no wonder everyone here will at some point come down with the plague. Maybe Kairos and Carolina would want to organize a trash pickup around the Arno, I think aimlessly. When I'm out of imminent danger, I make a mental note to talk to them about recruiting a bunch of kids to help.

Young urchin boys in tattered pants tag up beside me. "Shoo!" I shout again and again. They definitely disrespect a girl's personal space here; that's something I've noticed generally.

I keep moving, swinging my arms to clear my way, but the little beggars continue to follow me anyway. Shouting like banshees, they duck in close, whooping and hollering. Touching me, like I'm an alien creature or something. It gives me the creeps. I give them the look, and they laugh and scatter only to regroup at a distance in a huddle, evidently conspiring.

Suddenly, the littlest boy darts toward me and pulls up my cape—

maybe they're hoping I'm naked or something. Luckily, Signora Vincenzo's daughter's petticoats and skirts cover everything; it is no doubt the least fetching outfit I've ever worn! And the wool is so coarse; I have to say it itches like the dickens. (Note to self: Tragically, the actual Dickens, as in the author of *Oliver Twist* and other books about poor waifs like the pesky boys here, is not yet born.)

So allow me a fashion news flash: I have learned that Florence in the fifteenth century has a major textile industry, with the Wool Guild being foremost among them. Whilst the peasants and working people apparently couldn't afford the best quality woolens (hence my current itchy condition), Lorenzo and the gang sport the finest apparel the Wool Guild must turn out. (See observations above, re: widening inequality.) Needless to say, their every itch is scratched.

I have to grin, thinking what Beth would say if she could see me now. Or imagine Bethy stuck in this fashion disaster of a time warp. For the heck of it, I sneak out my phone and take a quick full-length selfie for the next blog post to Billy.

The sun is directly overhead, scattering diamonds of light off the river as I get closer. I hope it isn't a mirage. I take off in a sprint for the riverbanks, hiking my long skirt up to free my legs, thankful for all the practice my job as midfielder on the soccer team has given me to get in shape. The ankle still smarts, but at least it's not like before.

The boys point and tease, but I don't care. What, like they've never seen a girl's legs before? I mean, really!

"Olly olly oxen free; can't catch me!" I sing, as I leave them in the dust.

I get to the bridge and arrange myself to try to blend in as best I can. Merchants and farmers have set up their wares for sale on carts and wagons in a marketplace of crowded shops. I would've thought at this noon hour they'd be swarming with shoppers, buying stuff for their families' suppers—visiting the butcher, the baker, the candlestick maker—with even more on the Ponte Vecchio bridge itself. But instead, I see just a few older boys, maybe around my age—apprentices, no doubt—loafing in the noonday sun.

Siesta time, maybe, and lucky for me. I duck beneath the bridge to rest by the river and cool down in the shadows. For almost the first time since I've arrived in this backwater, with the exception of my walk in the moonlight and embarrassing exile to the barn outside Vincenzo's, I'm pretty much alone. I slip off my shoes, pull up my heavy skirts again, and plunk my swelling feet and itchy legs into the Arno. I'm that desperate.

I close my eyes for a moment, allowing myself to bask in the light breeze off the river. Here's a rare slice of heaven. "Ahh," I sigh. "I could stay here all day."

But my mind's racing. What would Billy be up to about now? Probably at the library. Wonder what Lex told everybody? I imagine he'd be like, "Not sure how, but Charley just disappeared into thin air. No clue where she went. But I *kissed* her SO BAD!"

And then Billy getting all mad at Lex. Then somebody would suggest calling my dad. Who'd call the whole stupid CIA, or something.

So it's not just the present danger—what with *il Magnifico* and all—that I have to worry about.

I should've gone to Italy with Mom, like she said. 'Cause an all-expenses-paid visit to twenty-first-century Florence, with a real bed and real Italian pasta—wherever it originated—sounds pretty good about now.

And the science fair? Sheesh. I mean, we could've *written* a report on Leo's time machine. But *nooo*! I have to go and prove time travel's possible. And make trouble across five centuries, for everybody.

But I can't give up on my dream now. I've come this far!

It's then I hear a ping coming from my backpack, like a text message—but how the heck?!

"got ur txt & blog. good ur safe. Parentals limiting texting, too much $$$. can't do video. phone not smart. whu'd u see?"

Billy must have seen my blog! OMG, it worked! I don't know how, and I don't care: We have a connection. A flood of relief washes over me.

It's dicey to just text him back—his parents might be checking—and we could only do video chat in real time, even if he had it. I can't recognize the time stamp on his text, because time is all mixed up here! And since I can't exactly set up whatever "real time" might be with home . . . maybe playing TeenWords, Billy's game app, is the way to go.

Safer to do encrypted messages anyway. I open up the game app, dim the screen to save power, and play the letters M-O-T-H-E-R, as in, mine. With luck, I can get Billy to run interference to find out for me what's really going on at home. But I expect it'll be awhile before he gets the message and can reply.

I listen closely as the loud bells on the *Duomo* strike twelve times. Wasn't Leo supposed to be here by now? Not fifteen feet above me, a butcher's boy in an apron smeared with blood shuffles down the grassy banks to dump out rotten cow entrails or pigs' feet—or whatever grossness they can't sell to unsuspecting customers—over the side of the bridge and into the river.

As the Arno races downstream toward me, where the animal waste might end up tickling my toes, I quick pull my feet out of what must be a proverbial meat soup of river water.

I glance back up the bank to see the boy amble lazily away, humming a tune and knocking his empty pail, clang-clang-clang, against the wooden posts of the bridge.

Life feels slow here. Maddening. I shade my eyes: no sign of Leonardo yet. For a genius, he sure isn't good at time management. I begin pacing. I go back to the messages on my phone and quick type a clue for Billy to find me, if connection is still possible:

"Miracolo. cu @TeenWords. gtg. C."

"La-la-la—lah, lah. La-la-la—lah, lah . . ." The melody comes floating with the breeze. I don't know who's singing; the voice is too far away. But it's definitely a girl's voice.

Surveying the riverfront, I spy a raven-haired maiden waltzing up over the embankment. Ribbons twine through the long black curls spilling out from under her loose veil. Something about her looks familiar.

Weird, I think.

Except I must've said it out loud. *"Veerrr-ed,"* she imitates, curling her lips so her teeth glare white in the sun. She pronounces the word with that same trilling *r* like Carolina's.

"Originale. Eheheh!" her gleeful giggle wafts in the wind.

This girl's definitely around my age. She has dark skin and dark— almost black—almond-shaped eyes. If it weren't for the loose white peasant blouse and rust-colored skirt that seems decidedly un–*Teen Vogue*, I'd say this girl looks suspiciously like Beth dressed in costume.

"Chi sei?" I imitate after hearing Translator. The whole Italian translation thing seems to be coming easier to me now.

"Eh, Carlotta, you must remember me. *Elisabetta! Della Taverna Vincenzo?"*

But all my brain hears is . . . "Beth?"

The Girl-Who-Should-Be-Beth reaches out and taps my shoulder. *"Ah, no, E-lis-a-betta.* The girl whose clothes you are wearing?" I peer down at the billows of rough fabric spilling out from under my cloak, and try to make sense of what she's saying.

"*Mia mamma* has been worried about you. Especially after Ser Leonardo requested I find you."

"Your mom?"

"*Si*, you do not remember *la scena*, this morning—in the kitchen . . . making macaroni?"

It flashes before me again—my humiliating attempt to demonstrate spaghetti-making at Signora Vincenzo's.

I squint at her face. An uncanny resemblance. I don't know why I didn't notice it this morning. But then again, I was suffering from time-machine lag . . . or something.

"*Ah, scusi, Elisabetta*. So, why are you here again?"

"Ah, but I am telling you. The Maestro sent me."

"Uh-huh. And I'm the Pope!"

"*Il Papa*? No. The Holy Father has not sent for you. I come for Leonardo . . . and Kairos."

I shake my head like a dog coming in from the rain. For a moment I feel as if I'm hallucinating, but the double vision persists: Bethy-then, Bethy-now.

"Oh, so this is one of your and Lex's tricks!"

Elisabetta looks mystified. "Why, I thought, perhaps, we might become friends!"

"Friends? Hah!" My laugh is sarcastic. "I've tried being friends with you, Beth!" I'm sure my face has turned red as a beet. "Anyway, I mean, thank God. Because I was thinking I'd actually gone back in time, and you would never believe what I have been through!" It all must be catching up to me, because I cannot stop laughing hysterically.

Elisabetta/Bethy looks around as if it is someone else I must be talking to. "No, *mia amica*, I am certain we have never met before this morning. But, Carlotta, I think I can show you how to act more like a lady! I saw you trying to dance the *saltarello alla piazza*. I could teach you to dance *piu con grazia*—a bit more gracefully. Then you could choose from any dancing partner in the *Republica*, as do I!"

With a flourish, Elisabetta then coyly pulls a white linen cloth from her blouse and offers one end to me, moving with graceful waltz-like steps as if inviting me to dance.

I sigh loudly. "I can't dance. Besides, I have things to do; places to go; people to see."

"Ah, but wait. I almost forgot—Kairos told me I was not to peek, but that this must come directly to you." She looks around suspiciously, making sure that none of those boys on the bridge are close enough to see, then bends over to hike up her skirt to her ankles, revealing a thin white chemise underneath. Whatever she expected to find is apparently not quite within reach under her skirts, though, so Elisabetta releases her hems and loosens the string of her blouse around her neck enough to reach a hand down the front, quite unashamedly revealing more than the hint of a breast as the blouse slips from her shoulder. She doesn't seem to notice the boys inching closer. She fumbles to loosen a slim leather pouch hanging from a belt that has fallen around her waist so that it's lodged under the waistband of the skirt—which she then solicitously leans over to hand to me.

I'm more than a little shocked at her lack of modesty—and a little jealous, too. Seems she is even more like her namesake than I suspected!

Clearly the boys are appreciating the vista; their wolf whistles cause Bethy II, as I will call her, to smile and curtsy in their direction.

"What are you doing?" I ask.

"But they are mere boys!" she exclaims. "They mean no harm."

"Sure, suit yourself, Bethy," I say half under my breath. "But you're flirting with danger."

"And you do not?" she asks innocently.

"What kind of girl do you think I am?!" I snap.

"What kind?" I can almost see the wheels spinning. "Why, a girl like me, of course!" she replies coquettishly, twirling her full skirts as both shoulders slip lower to rest seductively on her upper arms. She doesn't even try to pull them up again.

I wish I could be this free. But not today. Realizing I am holding the satchel she relieved from its hiding place, I open it and remove the slim silver tablet. My tablet. Reverently, I open the cover and press the on button, holding my breath.

Bethy II also seems breathless. "Kairos told me to tell you this: Your tablet should be full of energy, thanks to the noonday *sol*."

After a long, breathless minute, I see the screen light up, and the wake-up notes chime their welcome song. I let go a long sigh of relief. I have never been so thankful for modern invention.

Charley Morton may still be able to find her future.

XIII.

Spun in a Web of Deception

Beth II has been off flirting with the boys, so I don't have to worry about her peppering me with questions about the blog and Billy. But since we've established contact, I just have to find out what's going on at home.

> **Blog Entry #4. FYEO**
>
> _Even later, same STD._
>
> _Billy, now that I know that my attempts to reach you are not random digital "messages in a bottle," I feel so much better! Because it's not just homesickness (and, btw, homesick feels SO much worse than time-travel motion sickness!), but being kept out of the loop that's driving me crazy. I caught a glimpse of my mom talking on some video chat app to her friend Giuliana. Here in Florence, but there in your time, I mean. And she's keeping a secret!_
>
> _Billy, it's got me crazy worried. Is she sick? Dying? I have no way to check it out. So I'm begging you—even if you're afraid of getting in trouble (or getting me in trouble) with my dad for not listening about the whole Operation Firenze deal, you've got to get to my dad! I've gotta believe whatever secret_

Mom's keeping from me, he's in on. They definitely don't keep secrets from each other!

So if I'm in Florence and she's in Florence I've gotta be able to help her, whatever time really is! 'Cause I'm pretty sure she needs me right now!

Just by hitting the send button, I feel a little more relieved. For good measure, I look at TeenWords and see it's my turn again. Billy's posted G-O-T-C-H-A, over the H in mother. How he got away with a non-word like that, I'll never know, and a double word score in the process. Look who's getting competitive!

L-E-O are the letters I play, more for the message than the point count. As I finish my turn, Bethy II comes huffing this way with nothing less than a baby pig in her arms!

"Those boys, *cosi generosi!*" The piglet squeals and jumps out of her arms.

It's so cute! The little thing comes to me—I am like a magnet for animals—and, impulsively, I reach down and scratch its ears like it's a puppy. I feel a smile cross my lips for the first time in, well, eons.

"Hi, cutie!" The little creature rubs up against me.

"Your mouth—it shines!" Bethy II gasps.

"Yeah, braces. Cost of growing up in the 'selfie' generation." I'm guessing braces aren't the norm back in time here—and probably not even brushing, much less flossing.

"*Brrrraces?*" she repeats, mimicking my speech, flourished with an impossible trilling of *r*'s. "*Questo* . . . ?"

"Well . . . oh, forget it." Too hard to explain. I scoop the pig up in my arms, but it's so little, it wriggles out. "Do you have a name, little one?" The piggy runs back towards Bethy II.

"Uno nomme? No," she corrects. *"E' cena."*

I adjust Translator over my ears. *Cena* (a meal) isn't a word we learned in class.

"NO!" Bethy's thinking of this little guy as supper! I put my arms around him and squeeze. I could never eat this little friend, no matter how hungry I get!

"I'm naming him Wilbur," I declare. He strains against my arms as I try to grip him tighter.

"Vil-burrr?" she repeats, mangling the *w* and adding a long trill at the end.

I roll my eyes. "Like, *Charlotte's Web*?" An allusion that is obviously lost on her. The fact that I'm Charlotte and, like the spider, stuck in a web (of time), holds no meaning here. I wonder if this girl would be able to read it even if the book had been written. Which it hasn't yet.

But she should at least learn Charlotte's friend's name, if only to inoculate the poor, dear thing against begin made into bacon.

"Wilbur. Wuh-wuh-wuh . . . ," I repeat, and see her trying to process this alien sound.

She looks so funny, pursing her lips and blowing in imitation. Need to sneak in a photo—maybe I can Snapchat this later or post it to my blog for Billy to really get an accurate picture of Florence back in the day: the height of civilization side by side with its livestock.

"No capische, vuh," she concludes after a few tries. All the while, little Wilbur is snorting and squealing, running from me to her and then dodging us both. Bethy II and I weave back and forth trying to grab him.

Bethy apparently thinks this is great fun. "He's a treat for the festival of Mardi Gras. *Per Carnevale!*"

Leonardo mentioned Lent was coming. So it's close to Carnival time. *Carnevale.* Time travel as I've stumbled into it is obviously not a precise science. It got me the right year, right place, but different month than in real time. So the time machine's settings for seasons, months, days, and even hours may be asynchronous (a word with Greek roots for the word for *without* [*a-syn*] + *time* [*chronos*], it has to do with things not going at exactly the same rate as something else—like being out of sync) with our own.

I must share this observation with Billy. If he gets back to me in this lifetime.

Bethy II is looking at me expectantly.

"Cool, Elisabetta. *Er, eh, fantastico*, that is."

"Hey, where the heck could Charley be, anyway?" The voice now emanating from my tablet speaks perfect American English.

"Who's there?" I slap my hand over my mouth—I didn't mean to speak out loud.

"*Questo?*" Bethy II asks back, all wide-eyed innocence. But she must not have heard me because now Wilbur's running away, and she's off chasing him down under the shade of the bridge, and calling out to him in Italian, "Come, piggy, piggy!"

"Knowing her, she's probably out building the bridge to nowhere."

So the tablet's tuned in to the real Beth, former BFF. Either I'm hearing things, or I'm really going crazy.

I try unplugging my ears, but all I hear are Wilbur's squeals as Bethy II grabs him.

Get real here, Charley, I tell myself. But then I'm wondering which real is real.

My focus is again interrupted by hushed whispers.

"Or Charley's lost in space, or something. Anyway, who needs her!"

Nice, Beth. There's friendship for you.

"Or Lex either, for that matter."

Billy!

"Where is that Lex creep, anyway?"

So Lex is also suddenly MIA? I peek at my tablet, and there are Beth and Billy on video chat together from separate study carrels at the library.

"Mind your own beeswax," says Beth. "Say, Webhead, aren't you and Charley supposed to be working on your project this afternoon, too?"

"Yep, we are." Billy wears a worried look. "Working out the math for it right now."

"Read my blog, Billy. The new blog!" I scream.

"*Que passa*, Carlotta?" I glance up to see Bethy II carrying Wilbur over the hill toward a fort-like citadel tower a short distance above where I'm sitting. Apparently startled by my screaming, she must've stopped short; I can see the piglet, sensing his opportunity, squirming out of her arms and running down the embankment; Wilbur is heading straight for the Arno.

"Wilbur, stop!" I yell. He comes now in my direction, his little cloven hooves digging into mud and grass as he runs along the riverbanks. "You scamp!" I laugh despite myself.

Bethy II scrambles down behind him. "Scamp!" she mimics.

First Kairos, now Bethy. *Scamp* is the one English word these Florentines all pick up on.

"*Che c'è*, Carlotta? Did Kairos not fix your machine?"

"*Niente*, Elisabetta." I breathe deeply, hoping I've turned down the sound on my tablet. No use in Bethy II getting all up in my face about the voices.

"*Dio*, look . . . *banditos*! Coming for Wilbur!"

Bethy II falls for the diversion. "Oh no!" She hurries back to chase after her treasure. Seeing her again engaged in rescue operations, I turn back to the tablet. I actually seem to have a clear connection to my old life! I take off Translator and put in my old earbuds, turning up the volume enough so only I can hear.

Billy again. "Charley's a little preoccupied with stuff at home," he says, typing while he talks to Beth. Did he get the next blog?

Bethy the First chimes in. "Yeah. Lex's also a no-show. Looks like we're both being stood up!"

At that moment, somebody, somewhere starts blasting music— the Retro Pigs, I'd say, judging from the chaos of chords flowing into my ears.

Retro Pigs. I sense a certain coincidental irony in the choice of bands Lex selected to test out for his and Beth's science fair project: growing marigold seedlings to acid rock music versus classical. Or no music at all. Testing how music determines whether life flourishes or dies.

"Hey! You guys. Cut the music a sec. Something's gone really, really wrong!" A guy's voice comes crashing in above the music.

"Lex, finally! You are *so* on my bad list—" Beth says, turning.

Lex has a panicky edge to his voice. "Is anybody listening here? It's Charley—I told her I wanted to know about my future as a player for the Nats, and her time machine . . . it's . . . swallowed her down a rabbit hole!"

I inhale deeply.

"What the heck!" Beth interrupts. "Forget about Charley. You had me so worried, Lexy!"

"Hmm, I think I might have found it—if I can replicate this code Charley left. . . ." Billy is still absorbed in typing.

"Check TeenWords, dummy!" I whisper, excitedly.

If he's found the code—and it's the one Kairos downloaded—then he's on the right track. If I focus all my mental energy on budging Billy's distracted brain in my direction . . . we've always had a good bit of telepathy between us. Although Billy would point out there is no hard evidence to prove that humans are capable of mind-to-mind information transfer.

Billy jumps up. "This is it: the Qualia Rosetta!"

Good job, Billy! He's homing in on the secret.

"Qualia schmalia!" Beth looks underwhelmed by the import of his revelation. "The reality is, Charley's a serious attention hog. Watch—she'll show up just in time to grab the spotlight."

"The blog post, the texts . . . I didn't really believe it. It seemed like a big fat joke!" Billy is quiet for a moment. "So . . . she's actually gone and done it! Gone down the rabbit hole. Or more accurately, perhaps, she's entered a wormhole. If she was able to successfully activate the Qualia Rosetta. . . ."

"Yeah, qualia, that was the word!" says Lex. "So, do you have any idea where Charley could've disappeared to, Billy? Maybe she's posted on social media or something. We should check."

Touching, Lex being all worried about me.

Beth's looking at her phone now. "Her Facebook—must've showed up on her Twitter, too. Last update was something about your guys' project, Billy. Some weirdness about a 'golden compass' . . . and she posted a picture of a weird dude in a Halloween costume on horseback.

I bet she just went up to the stables at Wheaton Regional Park!"

"The key!" Billy looks up, as if something just dawned on him. "Where's the key?"

"Who said anything about a key?" Beth, suddenly suspicious, walks over within range of Billy's laptop. "Anyways, how come none of this seems like a surprise to you, Webhead?"

If I hadn't heard from Billy already, I'd agree he was being unusually Spock-like in his rational explanation of a situation that would otherwise seem to be pretty seriously out of whack.

"We followed the design, but I didn't really believe anything would happen. Once we plugged in the coordinates—I guess it's thanks to that Kairos guy—and based on the notebooks, I'd say we reached our target. Wow. This is incredible!"

Lex is pacing in and out of the camera frame. "Don't be so cryptic, Billy. 'Cause if we're gonna get in trouble over Charley's being missing and all . . . it's like, news flash: 'Brainy girl missing; future Nats starting pitcher to blame.' And that's the end of my baseball career!"

Seriously? I'm trying to navigate my way back through 500 years of history where I am not supposed to show up in the first place and may have completely rewritten history by accident, and all Lex can think of is his future baseball career? What the heck?!

But then, clearly, Beth and I are also on separate wavelengths. I take out my earbuds and grab Translator. If it can bridge the thought-language barrier, maybe time is no obstacle either.

Need one of them to get this thought in a mind meld: *Not kidding here. Stuck out of time.*

"Oink, oink, oink!" As something brushes hard on my gimp foot, I startle.

"Eek! *Dio mio*, you scared me!" I squeal back.

Bethy II and her dinner have once again caught up to me. The ancient Florentine version of my once-and-future BFF plops down next to me.

I quick slam the tablet cover shut again before a now-muddy Wilbur crawls into my lap, crushing my main link to home.

"Bethy, don't you want to dunk him in the river or something? I think Wilbur could use *uno bagnio!*"

"*Uno bagnio!*" Bethy II giggles.

This seems to trigger new attention from the boys, who come running at her laughter. Here for a pig hunt, I'd wager.

They keep edging closer and closer, as if on a dare.

This game gets Bethy II on her feet again. "*Ayiee!* Here we go again! *Viene con me,* Carlotta!" she calls back over her shoulder, trying to get me to join in.

It appears we are to be on the move. I look around for my shoes, anxious about squeezing my bad foot into the ballet flat over the ragged and dirty bandage. Seems I need not have worried—they are nowhere in sight.

"Wait, who stole my shoes?"

At that moment, down by the river, I hear a rebel yell—the little boys are looking back at us even as one brings back his arm, launching something into the river.

"No! MY SHOES!"

"Those scoundrels!" Bethy II says dismissively.

Of course, look who still has her boots on!

"No matter. We must get back. I will take you to Maestro da Vinci." She marches off at a clip.

Gathering my stuff together, I limp up the steep riverbank, trying to keep up with her. "Wait, Bethy! I'm coming!"

XIV.
Two Worlds Collide

"Where are we going now?" I ask, bedraggled, tendering bare feet over stones and dirt as we trek back into the heart of town. My gimp ankle is seriously hurting. Bethy II's holding the squealing Wilbur, exclaiming over her mamma's cooking. I am tempted to set the poor piglet free in a back alley along the way so he doesn't end up as bacon tonight.

As we pass through the center of town, I am seeing what I guess are shops and vending stands—the fifteenth-century version of a shopping mall. Except here, there are no price tags; everyone's haggling and shouting.

We end up at what looks to be a stone fortress in a busy Florentine square. *"Il palazzo dei Magnifico,"* Bethy II informs me importantly as we stop at its gates. She knocks at a guardhouse, and I have the feeling we're gonna be patted down, like airport security. Imposing-looking soldiers stand in full regalia, swords on their hips, and one matronly looking lady is wearing something a bit more refined than the customary rough peasant dress—the guardhouse mother, no doubt.

I pull on Bethy's arm to ask her whether we have to leave Wilbur outside and take everything out of my backpack for inspection— could the maquette and key be confiscated as potential weapons, I wonder?

Bethy just nods and gestures for me to follow her lead, proffering her cheeks to the guard for multiple kisses on both sides, then nodding to me. As we pass, I practice my fancy little curtsy again and manage not to fall flat on my face, a fact that Wilbur, no doubt, must appreciate.

"Viola's my mother's cousin," Bethy II explains, elaborately saluting the guards.

Is everyone related to everyone in Florence, I wonder?

We enter through a massive courtyard. I am dizzied looking right and left through columns and past trees as we wind our way along a path lined with the most amazing collection of Roman, Greek, and Renaissance statues in stone, bronze, and marble; clearly this is way grander than the sculpture garden outside the Hirshhorn Museum on the Mall at home. No wonder *Magnifico* keeps armed guards at the gates! But I have other problems.

"Where is Leonardo, anyway?" He promised he'd come find me— but that was hours ago already.

"We are to wait for da Vinci inside a private drawing room," Bethy II instructs, as we head for the smooth marble-floored entrance.

Inside, the palace takes my breath away. It is ginormous! I've never seen anything like the frescoes, heavy tapestries, embroidered bell pulls, and paintings that line every wall. I had no idea such treasures even existed outside a museum!

The crystal chandeliers have actual candles in them that flutter when the heavy metal door shuts behind us.

But it is the gilding on the walls and high coffered ceilings that really light up the room. My eyes float up to take in the walls, busy with paintings, sculptures—angels and cherubs, and so much gold leaf—so bright, that sunglasses should be handed out at the entrance.

"Wow." I can't even imagine the White House, the Capitol, and our Supreme Court together holding such treasures as this Medici palazzo. Even the ceilings are painted. It is nothing short of dazzling. You don't even have to be an art lover to appreciate the treasure here.

The gold marble floors shine under torchlight and are lined with

old Persian rugs and runners (apparently ancient even back then!). I'm almost afraid to walk on them; I hastily pick up my bare feet to make sure I'm not tracking in mud.

Apparently Elisabetta feels no such qualms: She sets Wilbur down, and he runs, squealing and grunting noisily, alongside us as she trudges forward, unimpressed by the finery, and makes her way down a long, dim hallway to await the Maestro.

"We must wait here," she says, pushing open a heavy, needs-oiling door that opens to what must be the grand ballroom. Dark wooden desks, every inch carved into menacing lions, gargoyles, and cherubs. There are gilded, overstuffed couches with intricate needlepointed cushions and gold-tooled leather ottomans. It once again seems pretty clear that the wealth divide is starker in Renaissance Florence than the difference between a Wall Street trader and a single mom scraping by with a job at Walmart.

And so is the difference in attitude. No one would ever set a pig down inside, say, the White House! Since Bethy II seems not to be concerned about destroying the antiques, and my foot is killing me, I plop down on a wood-armed, red-velvet-upholstered, striped-silk-pillow-festooned couch. But far from feeling swallowed up in kingly comfort, this seat turns out to be truly a pain in the butt.

My new BFF in this space-time zone has not stopped gabbing. "So, we wait . . . and wait. And wait," she huffs, annoyed in a way that reminds me of her twenty-first-century namesake.

I prop my foot up on one of the ottomans to rewrap the linen dressing. It doesn't look like the swelling has gone down much. I decide that maybe airing it out—the bandage is hot and really doesn't provide that much support (how long before we get to the invention of spandex?)—would be good, as long as we have to wait anyway.

The room takes my breath away. Every inch of every red and green and gold wall is molded and gilded and hung with massive framed masterpieces. The magnitude of what has been happening engulfs me. This story is *sooo* much bigger than me and a time machine. Or my friends being selfish. Or my mom being . . . whatever.

"What is wrong, Carlotta?" Bethy II asks, looking suddenly concerned. "Your face—so pale. Are you ill?"

No. Yes. Maybe, I think.

"Because I can understand if you feel unwell. Many pilgrims come here from faraway lands only to fall ill. It isn't so long ago that the Black Death was killing off entire families! Did you see the cemetery we passed? And those who came from afar were often weakened by their long journeys and could succumb easily to this terrible affliction, especially after the physicians bled them out."

"Are you freaking kidding me? You guys have a plague going on here now?"

I knew I should've washed my hands after handling Wilbur! I quick check the backs of my hands and arms for oncoming boils or blisters that could be a first sign of the dread disease. Because it is well known the Black Plague took a far worse toll on the population than any swine flu we might have running through the U.S. in any given winter.

"Oh, no. That happened before you arrived, by many years. Besides, I would not put you in the category of the weak, Carlotta!"

"Phew. 'Cause that's all I need is to catch the plague!" Apart from not carrying any antibiotics, the fact that doctors used to think disease was caused by bad blood—and would bleed out already sick people—makes no sense!

To be certain, I grab the tablet out of my backpack to search my history e-textbook for "years of plague; Renaissance, Italy," before I remember: future history, erased on viewing.

I keep staring at the tablet anyway, willing it to show me what is really going on—now, then, in whatever time I have left. All the things I took for granted: the convenience of looking up anything, anytime, anywhere. I have a gazillion questions about time—how to move forward and back at will. Kairos seems to have mastered this but is keeping that knowledge to himself.

And I know Billy knows where I am, but I wish he'd hurry up and help me out of this predicament. Or at least give me a clue about where I need to bring Leonardo up to speed so he can help get me home.

My eyes are tearing again.

"You look deep in reverie, Carlotta," Bethy II suggests unhelpfully, taking the dead tablet out of my hands. "Maybe it is the hysteria, then?"

"Hysteria?" (OMG, such an insult against women: In the olden days, hysteria was tied to "lady" problems; as in, our emotions cannot be trusted at certain times of the month!)

"Me, hysterical? Definitely NOT!"

"Because I, too, have suffered from the hysteria, Carlotta." She leans in, as if to confide a secret.

"I am to marry, a year from now. You may be jealous of my good fortune. He has property of his own, my intended. Massimo di Amore. And he is wise to the needs of women. After all, he has more than *trente annos*, and much experience!"

Actually, as Bethy's saying this, she doesn't look all that happy about it.

"He's thirty years old? You're kidding! I mean, why? It's not like you have to get married or anything, right? I mean, do you even love him?"

"Love? What has *l'amore* to do with it?"

"Well, I mean, shouldn't you love the man you are to spend your life with?" I crinkle my nose. "Besides, thirty is . . . OLD!"

"Oh no, you misunderstand! My one true beloved has no more years than I! You think I must love my betrothed? No, Carlotta, my heart belongs to Alessandro, a boy of my own age who was sent to Rome to take his vows and work for our Pope. He was a stable boy to *Magnifico*'s nephew, Giulio de' Medici."

"Alessandro is your true love!" This opens up the floodgates. "Mine too. I mean, I have a tiny crush on another Alexander. Lex. I don't want to marry him, though! Has he, you know, tried to kiss you yet, your Alessandro? 'Cause I'll tell you, Lex tried to kiss me in the garage and it was . . . well, transporting, is all I can say."

Elisabetta's eyes are closed and she apparently sees something rapturous behind her closed lids. "Ah, yes, Sandro kissed me and"—she opens her eyes—"*transporting?*"

"Well, yeah, it was like, so . . . unsettling. He had his arms around me with this weird look in his eyes. You know the feeling?"

"*Ah, si!* My beloved and I have met many times in the loft above the horses. When he holds me, it is as if the world is spinning!"

"Exactly—spinning! And weird lights . . . this music all around. I felt like I was wrapped in a cocoon of light. I was falling—"

"Yes, falling! I have felt this way, too!"

"And when I opened my eyes—no Lex. No garage. A loud *kaboom*, and a cannon ball whizzing by!"

Elisabetta looks at me oddly. It is suddenly clear, Translator or no, we are not speaking the same language.

"You are sure you feel *bene*, Carlotta?"

"*No si bene.*" But not in the ways Bethy II is thinking. No. Apart from all that small stuff, what's making me suddenly sick is this: Worse than worrying about my mom and missing my friends, maybe a cause for hysteria—I have interrupted the flow of history. What am I doing here?

A familiar voice interrupts my ruminations.

"No, my beloved. What do you mean Charley's missing? Didn't you arrange a pickup time with her at the library?"

Mamma must be speaking to Dad. Her voice sounds concerned.

"Who is here?" Bethy II jumps up, dropping the tablet onto the floor in the process. Music, snippets of dysphonic sounds, pulse into our ears—sounding ever so much like the tuning of an orchestra—horns blare followed by the sporadic thump of a timpani, the crash of cymbals out of sync with the sawing of the viola, and the tinkling notes of the piano weaving intermittently until they resound symphonically. Suddenly, Puccini.

Bethy II looks curiously at the dark square on the ground. "Oh, *Dio mio*! What angry spirits have you captured in your magic box, Carlotta?"

"Phew! I was worried that my tablet was dead!"

It's annoying that I have to explain this all to Bethy II. But I feel relieved, in a way.

I scoop the "magic box" up from the floor before Wilbur, hiding beneath the sofa, can trample it. Wish I understood how it was transmitting signals—and randomly switching locales from Florence to Takoma Park.

I lift the cover and see my mother's face looking very much alive. "I wish you could be *here*, here," I whisper to the screen.

"Gwen, I'm telling you all I know. I found this sticky note on my computer in the workshop. And when I tried to call her, her phone went straight to voice mail!"

"Dad!" I exclaim. He's video chatting Mamma now, apparently talking about a note of some sort. I gasp as he shows a close-up on the screen:

Don't worry, M. M. Charles's gonna be fine.
Getting her back in time. Will explain later.
Yours truly,
E.V.

Huh? I take this for Billy's illegible handwriting until I realize he's just being cryptic.

"Jerry, I can't really read that," Mom says, squinting her eyes from the lights where she must be backstage. "Wait, who—or what—is V. B.?"

Mom pauses, tapping herself on the forehead. "Wait, no, it's B. V. Looks like someone's tried mirror writing."

"Some genius, whoever it was!" Dad flips the note:

Don't worry, Mr. M. Charley's gonna be fine. Getting her back in time. Will explain later.
Yours truly,
B.V.

Bethy II gasps. "*Questo magico!* Phantoms speak. We must hie away! They will come for us, Carlotta!"

I sigh. "No ghosts, Bethy. It's just a box."

She cautiously creeps closer. "*Esta tua madre?* At the Palazzo Pitti?" she says, inspecting the setting behind my mother.

"B. V. would be . . . Billy!" Mamma exclaims.

Dad gets a little overexcited at this news. "Billy Vincenzo? He broke in here? Why, that little punk!"

OMG. They are totally thinking the wrong way about Billy. "Dad, you really don't get it, do you!" I try to tell him. "Billy's trying to rescue me!"

Bethy II's still staring at the screen, trying to figure out the foreign-sounding tongue without benefit of my Translator.

"But the *bella donna—la vostra madre?* I have never seen an instrument such as she holds in her hands. And all those others making this strange *musica?*"

I listen for a moment. In my excitement to see Mamma again, and hear Dad's voice, I had tuned out the fact that the orchestra is running through a familiar score: mine.

"*Mamma mia!* That's not Puccini!" I exclaim. "That's my song! The song I wrote with *mia madre!*"

"Puccini?" Bethy II repeats, looking confused. "This is a song of Firenze?"

Their rehearsal seems to be wrapping up now, for the noise has changed to the clatter of putting away instruments, closing cases, clasps clicking around their priceless instruments, followed by idle chatter.

"Jerry, I'll need to call you back—we're about to get notes. Do you think we should call the police? Has it been twenty-four hours yet?"

"Let's not panic, Gwen," my dad says.

"Have you checked her Facebook? Maybe there's a clue. After all, she can't have gone too far—and you should definitely track down Billy. He's some kind of tech mastermind."

"You know, Gwen, I'm sure there's a logical explanation—she's probably going to walk through the door any minute now. Would her friend Beth know anything, do you think?"

"Charley and Beth are on the outs at the moment. You know, teenage girls! Why don't you track down Billy Vincenzo. I'll see if I can contact Beth's parents." Mamma sounds calmer with a plan.

"Oh, Charley! Life would be so much simpler if she'd just follow the plan." It's almost like Dad could read my mind. Can he? I wonder suddenly.

I can see Mamma is talking, opening up her violin case, and trying to balance the phone all at the same time, without too much success. As she attempts to close her musical score with the violin bow, she knocks over the music stand—a Charley move for sure.

I hear a clatter and a big, long sigh.

"Gwen?" Dad looks concerned.

"I am such a klutz!" Mom exclaims. By the looks of it, her phone has dropped to the floor, and the screen blurs and turns to black—apparently, the bottom of a music stand.

Then a big paw closes over the camera lens as someone picks up the phone with a harrumph and hands it to her, but not before I catch a glimpse of his face. A young, dashing stagehand stares straight at me through the camera lens. A stagehand who looks rather astonishingly like Kairos.

"Kairos!" I gasp, and quick clap my hand over my mouth.

Too late—Bethy II is completely tuned in now. *"Kairos? Questo magico?"*

How could Kairos be there when he was just here? And how could he be talking to my mother?

"Scusi, Signora. I couldn't help . . . perhaps in this time I can offer reassurances. Is this *Bee-ly Vincenzo* of whom you speak not a member of the Florentine *famiglia Vincenzo?"*

Mamma, obviously not knowing who is speaking to her, hushes him.

"Kairos? *Dove?"* Elisabetta asks, looking around. "Kairos is the one who is to bring Leonardo the news of our whereabouts, Carlotta."

Again, I hear Mamma's voice. *"Prego,* Signor. I don't think you understand. My daughter seems to be missing!" She concentrates on the screen and starts pacing.

"Jerry, are you still there?"

Kairos comes into the frame again, holding a tablet of his own. He seems to be hunting and pecking on the keyboard, like he's typing a message.

It gives me another window into Mamma's world. Around him, I can see stagehands resetting chairs, moving around lights—all the things that need to happen before a performance.

"Signora! *Scusi*, but I know where to find—"

Then, Dad's voice chimes in, as if he hasn't heard any of that exchange. "Gwen, I just logged in as Charley and checked Billy's Instagram."

Thank God the parentals insisted on having my login for social media, I think.

"You are not going to believe this, but I believe Charley may have followed you to Florence!"

"This is what I am trying to say, Signora! Your daughter . . ."

"He's telling the truth, Mamma!" I can tell she's ignoring Kairos—or whoever he is who's doing an excellent impersonation. "Pay attention to him!"

"Florence! No, Jerry, that's impossible! Charlotte was distinctly uninterested in joining me on this trip, what with her science fair deadline and working with Billy—and Lex, the school's star baseball player. Whose effect on Charley worries me a bit, quite frankly."

Kairos isn't giving up. He goes over and clasps Mamma on the shoulder and enunciates each word slowly.

"Signora, this is what I am here to tell you!" He turns around his tablet and shows her something, but I can't see the screen.

Her mouth drops as the full import of whatever it is seems to sink in. My heart sinks as I see her face blanch and the blood drain out of it.

"Mamma? Mamma!" Why can't she hear me?

"Jerry?" her voice is no more than a stage whisper. I strain to hear her, cranking up the volume.

"Jerry . . . you may be right. It's Charley. At the Medici Palace. But not—" And just like that, Mamma crumples to the ground.

In a flash, there is a commotion as Kairos cradles Mamma under her shoulders, and other members of the orchestra crowd around to obscure what's on any screen—hers or Kairos's.

And with that, the world fades to black.

THE EDGE OF YESTERDAY:
COMING BACK TO THE CODA

(Coda: a musical term that is Italian for the ending of a song or a dance—but also, like, The Last Word.)

I'm dreaming, I know it. I have built a time machine spurred on by a drawing, a vision, and a school project. Somehow, it worked.

Inside my dream, I wake up in the deep past. Except it is now my present: 500 years until the present. I have no idea what my future holds, or if I even have one!

I revisit the facts: school science fair, found Leonardo da Vinci's plans for a time machine, but he didn't have technology or science to build it . . . but twenty-first century, different story. Blah, blah, blah. And since I'm determined to be a modern-day Leonardo, I'm the girl who's gonna prove time travel's not only possible, but I have made it happen! So I am sojourning (isn't that a good word? It means to reside somewhere temporarily. God, I pray that this is only temporary!) in a faraway past—1492, to be precise, in Florence, Italy, when it isn't even really Italy (and has somehow not caught on to the delectable tastiness of spaghetti and pizza yet . . . I mean, who knew?!). I have actually met Leonardo da Vinci face-to-face, and I don't mean an impersonator or, like, Leonardo Di-Caprio playing the Renaissance genius.

I AM NOT KIDDING.

And there's a whole lot of drama going on here! Like Leonardo is totally gonzo over my tablet that is showing him the future that he now is determined to invent. Including painting the Mona Lisa ('cause history says he won't actually start to paint it for another ten years). So we're talking time paradox here, and it's my fault.

And that's just the start! There's this preacher, Savonarola, who is totally anti-technology. In fact, he's convinced people they need to burn all the books, paintings, furs, jewels, and wigs, for God's sake, so people are gathering every day in the piazza of Florence to hear him speak, then heaping all their priceless possessions (imagine—we are talking about Michelangelo's sketches for his sculptures, Botticelli's paintings, and lots of jewels, furs, gold, and stuff!) onto a giant pyramid, thirty feet high, to be burned! A Bonfire of the Vanities, it's called. And, as Kairos so delicately pointed out earlier (ahem!), if this Savonarola dude were somehow to get wind of my tablet and phone (thank goodness I figured out how to make a portable battery to keep my devices charged!), he would no doubt turn me in for foretelling the future. A future, I might add, he would disavow as heretical if he were ever to live to see it. And have me burned at the stake. So, if his followers, the Weepers, catch me, I'm gonna be toast. Literally!

Meanwhile, back at home in my own time, my mom may be dying (how I have gleaned that fact from here is a whole 'nother story!); my science fair partner Billy and I are mysteriously able to communicate back and forth through an app he invented called TeenWords, and this whole thing seems to have been hacked into behind the scenes by this odd dude named Kairos who appears to be neither here, nor there, but everywhere and in both times at once!

Got that? Okay, me neither.

The good news—Leonardo is totally on board with my mission to reengineer time to help me get back home to the present. Er, the future. Or whatever. I have some new friends here, Elisabetta (or Bethy II), who is my age, and little Carolina, who's like this eight-year-old genius, who are a little behind the times (for our time, that is), but otherwise totally cool.

In spite of all the cool stuff that time travel has wrought, this Renaissance Florence is not a safe place. Book burnings, gypsy caravans that kidnap unsuspecting time travelers, bandits, Lorenzo de' Medici and his merry henchmen (NOT!), the filthy Arno River, no indoor plumbing . . .

I have no idea whether I will ever make it back in time to win the science fair, but we are not yet out of time!

Adventure of a lifetime? We have barely scratched the surface here. Now I know firsthand that time does not run in a straight line. And it is hardly predictable.

Do my findings contradict the laws of the universe? It will take smarter minds than mine to figure that one out.

Or maybe it's my destiny to be the one to prove the theory of parallel universes. That would be cool. If I have a future, that is.

Just in case, I am collecting evidence as I go.

For now, I am praying that my messages reach Billy in whatever future is happening centuries from now—hopefully one where I exist. And, mostly, I pray for Mamma to be okay. And for me not to have messed up history.

Because, frankly, it's all turning into one big, confusing, terrifying mess.

BONUS CHAPTERS
BOOK THREE

EDGE OF YESTERDAY: SAVING TIME

"It had long since come to my attention that people of accomplishment
rarely sat back and let things happen to them.
They went out and happened to things."

~Leonardo da Vinci

I.
Which Witch?

A sharp waft of ammonia mixed with awful perfume tickles my nose, followed by a burst of air. *"Achoo!"* I open my eyes—someone's waving this awful odor under my nose.

Did I lose it? When I come to, I hear many voices. I blink a few times—can't tell what I'm looking at. A domed ceiling painted with cherubim and shepherds and shepherdesses in a pale blue, cloudless sky. So I guess this would be heaven?

If so, heaven's far from sterile. Bethy II is fanning me with a feather duster; I don't dare think about the dust mites and allergens she must be stirring up.

"This foul-smelling alchemy could wake the dead," Bethy II is saying. At least that's what I imagine she's saying, given the stench. I am vaguely aware of being stretched out on the hard couch. Bethy's on a chair next to me and I need to figure out where I am, but my head starts spinning when I try to lift it.

"Oy! When did I pass out?"

"Oy? Che dice?" It's the woman from the guardhouse who let us in earlier.

"E mia madre?" I ask, hoping Bethy II will know something. Last I remember, Mamma had passed out at the Pitti Palace in another time

and Kairos was there, but I'm hoping that was all a figment of my imagination.

"*Sua madre! Viola, hai sentito che?*" squawks a woman's loud voice. I can't make out the words.

Where am I? I look around, dazed, and squint to bring the scene into focus, but it's all fuzzy. It begins to register that I am still in olden-days Florence, that Mamma is in future Florence, and all is not well in the world.

Why, though?

I turn to figure out the voice behind me—one that would appear to belong to Signora Vincenzo. It doesn't take twenty-twenty vision for me to see her point a finger at her temple and make a circular motion in what must be the universal sign language for crazy.

When did La Vincenza arrive?

Confusion notwithstanding, I push myself up on my elbows, biting back tears. "I want *mia madre!*"

But before I can gather my thoughts, the world begins spinning around me again, and Bethy II reaches out a hand to grab me before I collapse.

"*Ecco, Carlotta!*" Seems Bethy has somehow found Translator and is fitting it over my ears. "*È possibile't capire senza questi.*"

"Huh?" Though Translator appears to be working just fine, my ears aren't tuned in. My senses, it would seem, haven't quite connected with my brain. It's like someone's hacked into my head and completely rewired it.

As she resumes her fanning, Bethy II passes the feathers too close, and they tickle my face. "*Achoo!*"

"*Alla salute!*" says Signora Vincenzo. "*Non è principessa, Cleopatra che ha bisogno di voi il suo ventaglio!*"

Bethy II, looking confused, suspends her duster midair. "Cleopatra?"

I catch enough of this to seize on the name of the Egyptian princess, and my mind flashes an image of Cleopatra reclining on a barge floating on the Nile River, her servants fanning her with feathers like this one. So it's a fan, not a dust mop.

Her mother continues, "You know we will all catch our deaths if you continue stirring up this bad air, Elisabetta."

Bethy II lays the duster down beside me, close enough that I can more closely examine feathers that look to be plucked from an actual Big Bird. And I got to see up close and personal how ostriches are a real thing here. Then, of course, there's Leo's ostrich egg globe.

Who owned the bird that wore these feathers, and do they regrow? I marvel, staring at the low-tech feathered air conditioner. It's the only obsession that makes sense to my addled brain.

But having said brain affixed like this on trivia is keeping me from thinking straight. *"Achoo!"* I think I must be allergic to something in the room.

"Alla salute!" the women exclaim in unison. Somewhere nearby, Wilbur, the adorable little piglet I rescued from the fate of being turned into a pre-Lenten feast for the Duke di Medici and his hundreds of expected dinner guests, grunts.

"She's been a little strange," Bethy II chimes in, pointing to her head.

My newly unleashed-by-reason mind still streams irrelevantly, but my eyes begin to focus well enough to see that Bethy II appears quite the modern schoolgirl, wearing my backpack and sporting my earbuds.

Weirdly, she's picked up the fan and begins to shake it side to side, bobbing her head in time to something coming through those phones. What—or who—she's listening to is beyond me, but suffice it to say, it's probably not the Retro Pigs. Not the way she's got Wilbur sitting on her lap, so that when she isn't busy waving that fan, she's dunking her fingers in what looks to be milk—unpasteurized, of course, because Louis

Pasteur, who created the system to sterilize and kill bacteria and germs found in raw milk, won't even be born for another three hundred years or so—in a funky, antique blue-and-white pitcher on top of one of the expensive ivory-inlaid black walnut tables and allowing Wilbur to suck milk off her pinky. And giggling.

I sit up in a hurry, wondering if a persistent memory of seeing my mom talking to Kairos isn't just the remnants of some bad dream, when Bethy II stops and nudges Wilbur, squealing, to the floor.

"What are you doing, Elisabetta?!" What else of mine could she have misappropriated (definition: steal for reals)?

"Do not worry yourself, Carlotta. Your mamma is in good hands. I have been your ears for her," she says, pulling the earbuds off her ears.

"My ears! For Mamma—what are you talking about?"

"*La musica!* You fainted away before the bell tower on the Duomo struck two."

As she's speaking, I can hear the church bells chiming the half hour. So I was out for a good thirty minutes.

"Lucky for your mother, Kairos was able to find her help. '*A doctorrr in di 'ousa, a doctorrr in di 'ousa,*' he was calling!" I have to smile at Bethy II's attempts at recreating the English phrase she must've heard through the earbuds.

"And a *chirurgo alla Palazzo* then was able to cure your mamma. It was frightening, the needle he stabbed her arm with! But she's breathing *encorro.*" As she delivers this news, Wilbur grunts and snorts, trying to find his way back on to Bethy's lap.

What is she describing? A shot? They gave Mamma a shot? This would seem to confirm my worst fears. "Breathing again—was she—?! Where is she? I WANT MY MOTHER!"

It's like I'm speaking Greek. No one pays my words the slightest attention. They are all glued to the tablet as Bethy stabs the screen with her milky finger. I grab my tablet from Bethy II to see what everyone is looking at.

"That looks to be the *Palazzo Pitti*," Bethy says, inspecting the setting behind my mother.

"*Si*," says Signora Vincenzo. "From what Elisabetta tells me, we are the ones called upon to protect you from misfortune. *La bella fortuna* is on your side, Carlotta." Putting an arm around me, she attempts a consoling smile that looks more like a grimace.

I squirm out of her embrace and examine my tablet, hoping against hope the scene from the other side is still visible.

But *la donna* Vincenzo continues to hold my arm, intent on getting credit for her display of heroism in resuscitating me. "When my cousin Viola came running on the news from my Elisabetta that you were lying on the floor, suffering from the hysteria, I hied my way pronto here to the palazzo."

Wilbur nudges her around the ankles. "Who is going to take this runt home, Elisabetta? And how will we feed yet another mouth until this one is grown and fit for slaughter?"

At this, Wilbur runs a circle underneath the sofa and out between Signora Vincenzo's legs, almost toppling that formidable *donna* in the process.

Signora Vincenzo kicks him away unceremoniously and turns to me with what I can only guess are fake tears in her eyes. "Carlotta, this news has pulled at *mio cuoro!*"

A cast-iron heart, in my experience.

Until that Viola woman chimes in. "You are fools! With the French king close and a battle imminent, if said king were to capture this girl, and *Magnifico* to find his servant girl has been ransomed—"

"Servant! Me? Ransomed!" My tangled brain isn't sure which threat to find more horrifying.

"A king's ransom," nods Signora Vincenzo, embracing me now with newfound devotion.

"Not to mention the attentions of the Pope! As the good Friar Savonarola warns us, 'Beware of those without faith,'" Viola continues. "'We weep even for such infidels,' as the girl before us!"

The Pope! I think hard: Is this the time of the Inquisition in Rome?!

"But Carlotta is no infidel!" cries Bethy II in my defense.

But Viola's just getting started. "She attracts the wrong attentions. Savonarola himself has denounced the appearance of *una strega* in our midst. Don't you see? The omens she foretells with her magic slate—flying machines, future events . . ."

They think I'm a witch!

". . . as Leonardo himself shared with *il Magnifico* by way of warning!"

"Hold on, this doesn't seem right!" I cry out. "Leonardo surely wouldn't—"

"Then Lorenzo, in turn, implored Savonarola to reverse her prophecy to save himself from death."

"Me? Why would I want Lorenzo to die?" I implore, before remembering with a sinking heart that I had told Leonardo that this would be the year of *il Magnifico*'s death.

"And so it is . . . this witch casts her spell, and if her magic were to fall into the hands of the French, or worse, Pope Innocent through his spies, as some claim they have foreseen . . ."

A witch . . . a *witch*, they think I'm a witch! I can't get past that word! What did they do to women accused of witchcraft during the Inquisition? My brain's on fire trying to think my way through what this accusation could presage.

"Viola, surely you cannot believe the wagging tongues of the court," objects Signora Vincenzo, squeezing my shoulders. "She may be strange, but she brings no harm."

Vaguely, I wonder why the innkeeper's wife is suddenly being so kind.

"It isn't what you think, cousin," says Bethy II. "She is wise about useless things, but when it comes to affairs of the heart—"

"At least I don't go chasing after every boy under the sun!" I can't help but bite back.

"The secret to her knowing is no mystery, though," Bethy II says, as she grabs the tablet out of my hands.

"Bethy, no!" I scream, jumping up in panic. "Ooh, my ankle!" I feel my legs crumple again. Bethy catches me mid-fall.

"There, proof!" Viola exclaims. "She suffers for these crimes."

"Nonsense, Viola. She hurt her ankle in coming to the tavern." Signora Vincenzo glares at her cousin.

"Here, Carlotta, I brought something suitable for your feet, too." She pushes me down on the sofa, trying to shove my swollen foot into a peasant-style boot.

"*Youch*! You're hurting me!" I yell.

Apparently, this cry translates as distress in any and all languages because she stops shoving and allows me to pull the boot gently over my wounded ankle.

Again, Wilbur shows his snout, this time right under my foot. "Oh!" I cry, almost in tears. It's all too much!

"Shoo! Elisabetta, you'd best squirrel away this little pest before *il Magnifico* turns this sow into soap!" Viola scolds.

Sow! So Wilbur's a girl? Before this can register, *la donna* Viola turns her wagging finger back on me.

"And you! You will be punished—*il Magnifico* will not stand for his home being defiled so, thoughtless girl! Bringing pigs into this palazzo!"

Trying hard not to respond to the scold with something I will regret saying later, I busy myself pulling on the second boot. At least they'll give me a little more support, I think, once the hard part is over.

I carefully swing my leg out to admire Italy's finest. After all, the Italians are known for their leather, are they not? Hand sewn. Soft. The style's sort of like a cross between a lace-up moccasin and a bootie. Not horrible, I think, though I'm quite sure *my* Bethy wouldn't be caught dead in them. Side lacing, little fringy thing design-wise, leather sole—wouldn't help much on cobblestones, but still. Beats my flimsy slippers or those horrifyingly stilt-like chopines that I have seen on a few supposedly fashionable Florentine women tottering around the cobblestones. Talk about your accident waiting to happen! These are high heels in the middle, where the platform comes under your sole and arches up toward the heel.

I mean, could you see *me* attempting *that* balancing act?!

Come to think of it, maybe I already am. . . .

II.
Sorting Out Contradictions!

I complain to Bethy about needing to go to the bathroom-loo-WC-whatever they call it here. I mean, when a girl's gotta go, a girl's gotta go!

She points me to what is, literally, a closet down the hall where there's a marble bench that has a large hole in it (and who knows what's on the underside to catch the waste!), woolen towels to wipe, and a table with a washbasin and a pitcher filled with water. Stinks like too much perfume to mask bad B.O.

I wonder if I shouldn't squat, like Mamma's always saying you should do in public bathrooms. I mean, here they've gone through plagues, the pox, chlamydia (we had to study STDs in health class this year, and luckily, Mamma made me get the HPV vaccine, 'cause whoever would've imagined *this* scenario) . . . and who knows what else!

I try for the squat, but after a moment I realize that, for one thing, squatting on one foot is nearly impossible, and for another, I'm alone here, in private. I let go of any notion of delicacy I initially felt around this situation. For once, I'm glad I don't have to worry about female troubles of the monthly variety—I shudder to think of what options are available in this day and age for managing all that.

At first, it feels weird to bare my tush on the cold marble, but ultimately, I find it's more about trying not to fall in. And since I stashed my phone in my pocket, I can check my messages and maybe update the blog without many eyes watching my every move. They seem to be getting way too interested in my electronics. Besides, who knows the next time I might have this luxury without spies angling for evidence of my so-called witchy ways!

Truth is, I need breathing room. Whatever mess I've gotten myself into with this stupid time travel experiment—and whose idea was that?!—I need a way to process. And writing's always been my way to do that.

As soon as I log in to the blog, I notice a comment . . . Billy's!

submitted on 2018/04/12 at 4:10 p.m.
comment by Billy V.:

> *Charley, the kids are going crazy here: Lex gave some cockamamie story about you two in the garage and thinks he's gonna be fingered in a missing-person story and Beth's pretending she can't be bothered but I know deep down she's worried, and basically, I don't know what to tell them. That you've actually met the real Leonardo da Vinci? Like anyone's gonna believe me!*
>
> *Guessing to get you back in time the 2nd golden compass is gonna be important. You still have #1, right? Gotta figure out how to teleport #2.*
>
> *BTW, hard to read your posts—they seem to fade as soon as I open the Web page. Gotta save screenshots to read.*
>
> *Anyways, I biked over to your house to tell your dad . . . something . . . and no one was home. Luckily. 'Cause honestly, your dad's gonna be so salty . . . and he's gonna wanna know stuff I can't tell him, like how we got the stupid for-*

*mula! But I left him a sticky note on his computer where I'm
sure he'll see it.*

*P.S. U say u saw & heard your mom? Like a streaming video
or something? In ur next post, pls explain how/what. Could
use something like that in my new virtual world: Leonardo's
War Games.*

*P.P.S. Also, take pix 4 me: catapults, swords, cannons, armor,
soldiers. This is gonna be awesome.*

Well then! Bethy's worried about me . . . fat chance. Lex is worried
about his future with the Nats, and even Billy seems mostly concerned
about my bringing back images for his new video game. Some friends!
But I need them now if I needed them ever, because this new threat
sounds serious.

Blog Entry #5. FYEO. March 8 - CARNIVAL TIME?

<u>*Believe it or not, same STD.*</u> *Beginning to think time
makes no difference. At least not time as we think of it. The
campanile of the Duomo strikes here—hour, quarter hour,
half hour. Another clock on a different church—an alley and a
sculpture-filled piazza away—chimes the same hour, quarter
hour, half hour, but starts and ends moments later. The net
effect is that some clock somewhere is almost always sounding
off. It is total cacophony.*

*I think I'm obsessed with time because I am SOOO out
of it. But then, somehow I can see you through time—and
Mamma, and even Kairos, who seems to be literally everywhere at the same time—but you are in a different space-time*

plane, going about your day, same as always. Mind-blowing.

This place is nuts. Their so-called Republic is really anar-
chy! Rules make no sense—pigs running around palace floors.
Il Magnifico's like an Oligarch. The Pope may be on a witch
hunt—for me!

Urgently in need of key that reverses formula or death may
be my destiny here. And a super-duper battery. Any hints on
speeding the process of fission from radioactive decay, for ex-
ample? Sun power from here insufficient.

Also, do you have the other golden compass and is there
any way to teleport to my time zone now? Think it may take
two to un-tango the complications of massive temporal dislo-
cation.

Your PITT.

As I am typing, the now-familiar specter of other-time voices seeps
through the phone. This time, Dad.

"Yes, thanks for letting me know. No, I did *not* know anyone hacked
into the system."

Hackers? Would that mean me and Billy?

I open the video chat see if there's video with the sound. Dad's
standing in the garage, looking more than a little forlorn. His workshop's a total mess—like a tornado's torn through there. I guess the
energy transmission that created momentum for my trip out of that
world stirred up quite a bit of dust. I can see what remains of our time
machine behind him on the workbench. Not a pretty sight.

"What I do know is my daughter has vanished into thin air, which
apparently has to do with a boy and a school project, and my wife is
going to—"

This news is both scary and hopeful. Scary, 'cause I'm gonna be in

BIG TROUBLE if I ever get home alive. Hopeful, 'cause even if I am grounded for the rest of my life (which I think I might happily agree to at this moment), it can't be nearly as bad as being burned at the stake. No, but seriously—!

"What's that, Viola?" Dad asks.

Viola! *Impossibile*. Too many paradoxes here—Elisabetta and Beth; Alessandro and Lex; Billy Vincenzo, and Viola:—it's creepy. Would these have already been disturbances in the space-time continuum if I hadn't jumped the veil, so to speak?

"I don't know of any video games that would open spontaneously on that computer. *No one* is to touch any of the secure files on Operation Firenze. Let me check the remote network interface. Yes, hold on. . . ."

I see Dad rummaging around his workbench, searching through drawers. The banks of remote servers still seem to be doing their usual blinking and beeping. Nothing seems amiss to my eyes besides the mess that would really implicate me and Billy in criminal activity, or so I pray.

Dad stamps his foot. "Where's the manual. Don't tell me, they've taken the manual . . . CHAAARLEY!

"Oh, crap, I can yell all day and she won't hear me." I've never heard Dad cuss before. He seems to be listening on the phone again. "No, no need to call the police, Viola. I have a feeling it's no more mysterious than a science fair experiment run amok.

"Um-hmm. Yes, I get it—protocol. Sure, I will definitely file the report on this. Thanks, Viola. You bet my daughter will be answering to me on this one . . ."

I see him hang up the phone and plop down on his bench, looking dejected.

". . . as soon as I find her."

Someone's knocking, bringing me back to the present—this other present.

"Carlotta? *Hai fatto cadere in?*"

I clap on the Translator. "No, I did not fall in, Elisabetta."

"Good thing, because *il Magnifico* is screaming and cursing."

Probably demanding my head. "I think I'll stay in here then, *grazie*."

"But Leonardo, he also calls for you."

Reluctantly, I pocket my phone once more and emerge from the WC gloomily imagining what it will feel like to walk to the gallows or, worse, be burned at the stake. At least death by decapitation is instantaneous.

Bethy II understands none of my predicament, of course. As she leads me down the long hall to where the Masters of the Renaissance are no doubt waiting to pronounce judgment on one less-than-masterful girl, she natters on about her complicated love life. As if such girl talk still mattered. And yet, as my only girl friend here, I am beginning to treasure her confidences. In a strange way, she makes me feel more like a girl who belongs.

"Oh, but you know Sandro is a man of faith, not war! Though he promised, his vows to the Church mean nothing. He has pledged me we will consummate our love when next he visits."

Despite myself, I can't help but be a bit shocked by this admission. "And he's a priest? But the whole celibacy thing . . . that doesn't bug you? And you're like ready, you know, to sleep with him?!"

"Sleep? What has sleep to do with love?"

"Well, I mean, not exactly sleeping but, well, like, do you already know him well enough to . . ."

"*O, si*. I have known Sandro since we were but children hanging around the stables."

Whoa, talk about paradoxes! They demand strict adherence to the rules, except for the exceptions. Priests have girlfriends. They boast great advances in education but intolerance for new ideas. Extreme wealth side by side with extreme poverty. A flowering of art and beauty, along with enough ugliness of spirit to destroy it.

In the midst of all that, it's even more of a wonder that Leonardo could emerge with his superpowers for art, invention, music, engineering, science, math . . . and I thought pursuing the whole "Renaissance girl, master of learning" thing was tough for *me*!

But Bethy II here seems to find no contradiction in the idea that her boyfriend could be a priest, or cardinal, or whatever.

"So then what's the deal with the old dude?"

"Massimo? It is so complicated, Carlotta. My father's health is failing. He can no longer work and cannot pay the loans he owes the de' Medici for our purchase of the *taverna*. It would take a lifetime for a tenant farmer like my father to save up his own money—or make enough from the few florins we earn from lodgers—to buy what must sustain our family! Ser Massimo has offered to pay off our family's debt in exchange for my hand. It was the only way we could keep our lodgings here in Firenze. If I do not accept his hand, my sisters and I will be sent to a convent and my parents will be left with nothing. I cannot allow *mio pappa* to die dishonored."

That's a sad story. "Sorry, Bethy. I bet your dad's gonna get better!"

When I look up at her, Bethy's got a big, fat smile on her face. "*Si*. It will help *mio padre* to be rid of this burden. And I will still be allowed to see my beloved when he returns with Cardinal Giulio!"

The whole husband-father-boyfriend thing still doesn't sit right with me, but I have to admire Bethy's family loyalty, and her concern for her dad. Especially under the circumstances. Especially since I may have screwed up my own dad's life, big-time. "Tough choices, for sure," I concur, shaking my head. "And I thought giving up Facebook time to practice my music was a sacrifice. What you're doing is amazing, Bethy."

"Face book? *Uno volto folio*? Oh, how I wish I were lettered, that I could understand these things!"

The hallway turns and we are walking past what has to be a kitchen, 'cause I can feel heat from the ovens, and whatever's cooking smells so *delicioso* it sets my tummy a-rumble.

"Say, Bethy, I know they're like, expecting us ASAP and everything, but do you think the kitchen here could whip me up, maybe, a pizza? I'm really hungry!"

Elisabetta looks quizzical. "*Questo piz-za?*"

"Aww, man! Don't tell me you don't even have any *pepperoni* in Italy yet! *Mozzarella?*"

"*Ah, si, fromaggio. Momento.* We must await a time when *il cuoco* has gone to market. Cook does not permit strangers in his kitchen."

Seems like Florence's openness in this age of rebirth may not extend past its riverbanks.

We arrive back in the grand salon, but *il Magnifico* and Leonardo are nowhere in sight. Neither, for that matter, is Signora Vincenzo or Viola. Nor is there any sign of little Wilbur.

"So what's the deal here, Bethy? You yank me from my private sanctuary—to wait?"

"Oh no! Kairos assured me that they would be here!"

"Kairos is . . . *here?*" Last I could conjure, he was in present-day Firenze reviving my mom, who, I pray with all my heart, isn't dying.

"*Naturalmente, no!*" she replies. "*A qui.*" She reaches for my tablet, which I had stashed under my backpack, and opens the cover.

I grab it from her, and there is Billy's face. Before I can yell at Bethy II to stop being so nosy, I am absorbed into a different drama.

Billy's in his room. I can hear music playing in the background. Sounds like a Simon and Garfunkel tune. Figures he'd be listening to oldies. I hear him reciting the lyrics, "For Charley, whenever I may find her. Whenever I may find her. Whenever I may find her," almost like a mantra. It's touching, really. And reassuring.

He's got his tablet open on his bed to TeenWords, and he keeps checking, like he's waiting. I realize it's my turn to play: POSITION-FIRENZE. He plays the word ANNO, to which I append MCDXCII.

"I know, Charley. I get it. I need specifics!" I see his move: COORDI-NATE. I toggle back to the video chat screen and—whoa, people: Billy has left the room!

EDGE AfterWords

Edge of Yesterday is more than a book—it's a multimedia experience! Take it from me (Charley), there's a whole lot more to this adventure than what you read.

We've gone online to include YOU in the story at

edgeofyesterday.com

YOU CAN

- Get a sneak preview of my upcoming adventures
- Read interviews with some of my Heroes of History (like Albert Einstein)
- Find out how to learn like a Renaissance genius
- Pick up badges and stamps, as my adventure continues beyond Renaissance Florence to destinations in other centuries, to meet other Heroes of History (we may even travel to the future)
- Along the way, ask me anything about time travel . . . or just life in general. After all, I've experienced life as a teen in more than one place and time!

Expand your world. Explore other worlds. Share your dreams.

And share your journey with friends. Don't be trapped in one place in time—come join me today!

edgeofyesterday.com and **edgeofyesterdaybook.com**

ROBIN STEVENS PAYES is a social marketing consultant and science writer specializing in reaching—and decoding—teen brains. She dove headfirst into parenting teens when her three kids were trying their wings and testing their limits.

Since her passion is storytelling, she relished listening in on back-seat conversations between her children and their friends. As her kids grew, Payes tuned in to how their language, ideas, and attitudes transformed along with their bodies and brains. The exercise represented a complete anthropological study in teen social psychology. For a mom, teens may be lovable and exasperating, but for a writer and science interpreter? Priceless.

Payes lives in Rockville, Maryland, where she works with teens on STEAM learning—science, technology, engineering, arts and design, and math—and consults with readers on creating new apps, games, and story lines. Her grown children still engage in "backseat" conversations—but now she's the one riding in back. This is her second book for teens.

CPSIA information can be obtained
at www.ICGtesting.com
Printed in the USA
BVHW07s2228041018
529258BV00002B/19/P

9 781937 650933